The Forever Partner

Suzie Ivy

To my Granddaughter Shaylee
She's ten-years-old and read The Forever Team, fell in love,
and warmed my heart when we talked about the book. I may
have a budding detective on my hands.
This one is for you, Shaylee!

Chapter One

Death Before Sunrise

A techno rendition of Beethoven's 5th Symphony blares suddenly into my quiet bedroom. "Da da da daaaaa." My groggily whispered, "Crap!" is barely heard over the chorus while my fingers fumble for my cell phone. The too-bright screen shows 03:22 on Saturday morning, my usual sleep-in day.

A muttered "Yeah?" into the receiver is the best I can do before sunrise and coffee.

Bell, short for Belladonna, my K9 black lab partner, growls softly from the foot of the bed where she sleeps. She doesn't like being woken up either. Her sleeping on my bed is a problem but not one I'm willing to tackle this decade. When it comes to Bell, I'm a softy.

The dispatcher is disgustingly chipper. "Officer Franks is requesting a detective at a death scene, and you're up," she says. Ugh. It's my weekend rotation. I made homicide a year ago and I love it. We're a midsized town and have a small number of detectives. Previously, I'd worked as a street detective— theft, burglary, and domestic violence, with a sex crime here and there. Homicide is the meat of the department in my opinion, and I accepted the promotion gladly.

"Okay," I mumble before going silent, waiting for the gears in my brain to tumble into place. "Who's dead?" I finally ask, wondering if I know the person.

"Out-of-towner. Female guest at the motel."

I'm now awake enough to register it's not a local. "I'll be there in fifteen," I respond and end the call.

"Come on, Bell, you need to do your business before we go to work." I don't get a growl this time. Bell understands the word "work," and she knows her job. We've been together for two years, and we read each other's minds all the time. "There's a death at the motel," I tell her while grabbing my holstered gun off the nightstand. "I really need sleep right now," I add.

She doesn't answer; she's stubborn like that. I lead her to the back door and let her outside while I focus on what else I need to grab. She has a doggie door but I secure it at night and when I leave the house.

My basic evidence kit is in the trunk of my car, but the large duffel that may be required is in my office at the department. I open the closet door and grab my cold weather bag. It consists of everything needed to dress and walk out my door in under ten minutes. The bag goes with me to scenes in the winter months and contains essentials like energy bars and bottled water. My bulletproof vest rests in the bottom. In the summer, the bag has extra water for Bell and a sports drink for me if it's really hot.

I head to the bathroom to put on my clothes, brush my teeth, and throw my hair in a ponytail. When I enter the living room area, Bell is standing at the back door, waiting patiently. I take her harness and leash from a hook next to the door, let her in, and get her dressed. She's hopping around with excitement.

"Bell, sit. Stay." I usually don't need to give these commands, but she's been bored. Since I moved to the homicide division, Bell doesn't get as much action. She's highly trained and extremely expensive. I work with her regularly and keep up her training certifications. She's cross-trained on explosives and personal protection. Her job is to give her life for mine or my fellow officers. My last K9, a Rottweiler named Suii, did just that.

My eyes go to the mantel above my fake electric fireplace. Suii's ashes are contained in a wooden box with an inscription.

The heart and soul of a K9 lives forever.
His four paws enjoy the path of endless walks.
His food bowl is always full.
His fearless sacrifice never forgotten.
Rest in peace, Suii.

I know the words by heart. I mentally shake myself. Thoughts of Suii make me sad. I miss him. Bell and Suii are worlds apart, and Bell is no replacement for my former partner. The thing is, Bell found her way into my heart quickly and filled the hole left behind at Suii's death. We need each other, or so I tell myself.

When I took the promotion to homicide, it was under the condition that Bell remained my partner. No one argued. Pre-Suii, my reputation at the department wasn't good. My one and only partner died of cancer, and I became noncommunicative, downright grouchy, and impossible to work with. My sergeant came up with the idea to pair me with a K9. I always wondered if it was a joke that accidently worked out. No matter the reason, Bell and I are forever partners.

With Bell's leash in hand, I walk outside with eight minutes to spare. It's cold but no snow fell overnight. The dark windows of my police issue SUV don't need scraping which makes this early morning call-out easier. My old car was fitted with a K9 cage in the back seat, but the SUV has more room for Bell, and we were both happy when the trade for my new vehicle was made.

I load Bell into the back and give her

head a quick pat. She licks my hand, and all is right in the world. With a solid slam, I close the hatch and get behind the wheel. Without giving the engine time to warm, I pull out and drive to the one motel in town. There are two other fancier hotels, but their crime rate is low. The motel attracts hard-working seasonal power plant employees. On the other end of that spectrum, it attracts drug users with no place to go who need a cheap room or place to deal from. They also steal everything that isn't nailed down. When I worked property crimes, the motel was a hub of illegal activity, and a week didn't go by that we weren't called for something.

I navigate through town, seeing no one on the cold, dark streets. Without traffic, it's a ten-minute drive. I turn into the far west entrance of the motel and notice about ten cars in the lot. Officer Leonardo Franks, Leo to his friends, is standing next to his patrol vehicle, the overhead red and blue LED lights flashing silently. He's a good officer, came out of the drug task force a few years ago, and I'm glad he's the one on duty this morning. In his early thirties, Leo is everything his Italian heritage gave him—dark hair, olive complexion, strong jaw with a great smile to enhance his facial features. He also likes my dog.

Leo can display a scary scowl when needed. Since my partnering with Suii and then Bell, I'm finally fitting in with most of the officers and detectives in the department. I've used Leo's help on a few cases, and I've seen what his scowl can do to hardened criminals. You don't mess with Leo. He also has a soft side, and if you cooperate without giving him trouble, he handles his job with compassion even if he can be a pain in the neck.

My eyes quickly adjust to the strobe lights, and I notice a head in the back seat of Leo's vehicle. I sigh and give myself a mental shake. This doesn't look like my hopes for an accidental overdose are going to manifest. My slowed adrenaline spikes slightly.

Bell and I won't be playing fetch anytime soon.

Chapter Two

In Plain Sight

L eo saunters my way in that distinctive style that screams cop. I move slightly behind my SUV so we can speak out of earshot of Leo's passenger.

"Whatcha got?" I ask after a quick handshake.

Leo nods to the hotel room door in front of his vehicle where his headlights shine. "I was called out at three. Mr. Ledmen," he nods toward his vehicle this time, "called 9-1-1 because his forty-five-year-old spouse wasn't breathing and he didn't know how long she'd been dead. When I arrived, I checked her pulse. Rigor was setting in, so my best guess is two to four hours ago for time of death. I found something suspicious and had dispatch call you. Ledmen said his wife was drinking last night and passed out on the floor—"

I hold up my hand, palm out. "Don't feed me your suspicions yet." If his suspicions came directly from Mr. Ledmen, this would be different. Leo found something in the room, and I want to find it on my own. "Did you mess with my crime scene?" Yeah, I notice his slight grin. When it comes to my crime scenes, I'm not a nice person.

His hands go up, palms out. "I touched the body to check for a pulse and lifted one arm. I had Ledmen stand outside the door while I walked through the room. I gloved up and didn't touch or move anything."

This is one of the reasons I like working with Leo. He understands the importance of securing a scene. I look around the motel again. "You're taking second on this. Write your initial report, and I'll take over. Who has the shift after you?"

"Denise."

"Call her out early. I want her sitting with Ledmen at the station. We need him out of here. Did you notify Sergeant Spence?"

"No, he's out of town so I figured you would want to call the chief yourself. I'll have dispatch get Denise en route. Do you need me to have anyone else called out?"

"No," I say, deep in thought. "Not until I know what we're dealing with. I'm sick of rumors leaking from the department. Cops with flappy lips aren't my thing. I'm glad you're my cop on duty." I think for a moment. "Have Denise pick up the large evidence bag from my office before heading here. It's in the corner behind my desk."

Leo grimaces over the first part of my statement. He understands exactly what I'm talking about when it comes to rumors. Cops talk to their spouses. Their spouses talk to friends at church. Within an hour, the entire town knows or thinks they know every detail of a case. Those details are always skewed or downright wrong after being passed through several lips and ears. The end result is a blistering headache.

I pull up the chief's number on my cell and receive no answer. It's what I expected, and I leave a message. Adhering to policy by notifying my chain of command is covered.

I also call Sgt. Spence's cell. It goes straight to voicemail. Next, I dial Gabe Macky, our other homicide detective.

"Hey, Gabe," I say when he, too, doesn't answer. "I'm putting a dent in your time off. Sorry, but you know it's what I do best. I've got a suspicious body at the motel, and if it turns into a homicide case, Leo will be my second. Call when you can." I will run my findings past Gabe after I know what they are. When it comes to homicides, Bell has little to say on the subject. Gabe and I might not officially work together, but we have no problem sharing info and asking the other for help if we're stumped on an investigation or as is usually the case, making sure we cover all angles. Gabe understands male and female brains work differently. Sometimes he picks up on things I don't see and vice versa. If I didn't have Bell, Gabe would have been someone I could work with, at least now. Pre-Suii, no. It wasn't that I was the Lone Ranger; I was the angry Ranger, and Gabe stayed clear like most others at the department.

I disconnect and walk to the back, passenger door of my SUV where I stow my small evidence bag. It goes over my shoulder. I carry it to the motel room door and lay it on the cement.

"Denise is on her way; what do you need me to do?" Leo asks after ending his phone call.

"Turn off your top lights before the town stirs. It'll cause less commotion when morning traffic picks up. Hopefully, we can keep this low-key for now. I want Mr. Ledmen out of here before we start. I'll have a word with him first, though. After he leaves with Denise, run crime scene tape from pillar to pillar in front of the room to define our inner scene. Run another line of tape about twenty-five feet out. No one gets past the outer tape without my say so. Got it?"

I flip the switch to my digital recorder and place it in my left hand while Leo turns off his overhead lights and unlocks the back seat of his patrol car. Mr. Ledmen isn't in handcuffs, and I appreciate Leo even more. If there is a chance Mr. Ledmen killed his wife, I don't want him knowing Leo suspects it. I haven't examined the crime scene, but I trust Leo. His suspicion means something is off and needs a closer look.

Mr. Ledmen's eyes are red with wet streaks showing on his cheeks. This tells me nothing. People cry or they don't. Everyone handles grief differently. Lack of tears doesn't prove guilt and gushing tears doesn't prove innocence. I have no intention of questioning him fully until we're in the department's interview room.

I quickly assess Mr. Ledmen. Medium wiry build, no gut, he's fit. Short blond hair, neatly cut, green eyes that are looking at me in question. Most women would consider him nice-looking. I put my right hand out. "I'm Detective Laci Jolett. I'm sorry we're meeting under these circumstances." He grasps my hand and gives his name as Carl Ledmen, his grip firm. "What's your wife's name?" I ask gently.

"Mary, Mary Ledmen," he says softly after releasing my hand and looking down into his lap.

"I'll be handling your wife's case. I'll need to talk to you and get a full statement after I see to Mary. I have another officer coming here to drive you to the police department. It's warm there, and you'll be more comfortable. We can provide food and coffee if you need it."

He looks up from his lap, his voice barely above a whisper. "I know this doesn't look good. We had a fight last night. I can't believe she's dead. I need to call my family. My cell phone is in the room, and I don't have phone numbers without it."

At this point, my brain is alphabetizing facts and storing them in neat little braincell file folders. "I can't remove anything from the room at this time. If possible, I'll bring your cell with me and give it to you before we talk." From the corner of my eye, I notice another squad car pull up. "Officer Bullock just arrived, and I need to speak with her. She'll be able to help you with whatever you need until I'm available."

I closed the door and walked away, then discreetly turned off my recorder. Denise is in full uniform, and I realize I should have had her come out in civilian clothes. It's always the small details that cause trouble. I don't want Mr. Ledmen feeling threatened more than he already is. Uniforms intimidate, it's as easy as that.

As I near Denise, I asked, "Are you ready for this?"

She's been with the department for a little over six months. This is the first time I've included her in a death investigation. Sitting with a witness or suspect is never fun, especially when it can be hours before an actual interview takes place. Thus, the perfect job for a rookie.

"Whatever you need," she says with bright eyes. She graduated the academy shortly after her twenty-first birthday. She's five one to my five three height. She keeps her red hair short and off the collar. I met her before she left for the academy when her hair was full and long. She told me keeping it up became too big a problem so she decided to cut it. With her slightly round face and freckles, she looks like a pixie. She also looks entirely too perky at this hour of the morning.

I really need coffee.

"You might not like me after this assignment," I tell her honestly. "I need you to stay with Mr. Ledmen at the station. I'll be examining the scene and opening an investigation. Take him in and make him feel comfortable. If other officers or town residents call the department to see what's going on, you know nothing." I lean in a little closer. "No rumors will leak out on this case. Don't talk to friends or family if you want to be included again." Handing over my recorder, I explain. "Use this. Don't ask questions about his wife or what's happened. The recorder is set on auto and will record when either of you speak." I hit the red record button before handing it to her. Mr. Ledmen might volunteer information, and we'll have it recorded. Remember everything you say is admissible in court."

She nods and looks me in the eyes. "Yes, ma'am. If anyone calls, I know nothing." She shrugs. "I actually don't know anything."

"Mr. Ledmen is not under arrest. I don't want him feeling he's being detained. He needs to feel we're providing a safe place while we do our job. Put him in the front seat of your car and introduce yourself as Denise after I give your name as officer. It will help him relax if you can keep it informal. If you need food, call Sheila and have her to pick something up." Sheila is our lead record's clerk and the chief's assistant. She keeps her mouth shut and has no problem helping on weekends if needed.

"Yes, ma'am." Denise knows I hate when she calls me ma'am but even six months out of the academy, I know it's a hard habit to break.

"As of this moment, this is a homicide investigation, and Mr. Ledmen is a person of interest. It might also be accidental. Remember your officer safety and keep your eyes open. One more thing, don't say yes ma'am in front of Ledmen."

Her face reddens. We walk back to Leo's vehicle, and I make introductions. Denise plays her part to perfection. Before we transfer Mr. Ledmen to Denise's vehicle, I explain Denise will search him due to our civilian ride-a-long policy. Not quite the truth but no way will I allow him to ride with Denise if he's possibly carrying a weapon. I'm also fairly sure Leo searched him. Safety keeps us alive. Denise pats Ledmen down and nods to me when she's finished.

Standing close, I judge Ledmen to be six feet tall. I crane my neck to see into his blue eyes. They tell me nothing. We get him situated in Denise's car, and she pulls away.

It's time to find what triggered Leo's instincts.

Chapter Three

Initial Walkthrough

Motels are one of the few places I'm not required to obtain a search warrant. I can investigate a crime scene as long as there's no suspicion the hotel owners and/or employees are involved. However, I know the owners, and I've helped them many times.

Sveta and Feodor Ivanov are Russian transplants. How they ended up owning the motel is unknown. Feodor's accent is heavy and difficult to understand. Sveta's English is better. She also controls the family dynamic so she's the person I normally speak with. I enter the unlocked front office knowing a buzzer is going off in their rooms located through a door behind the front desk. The office looks and smells like motels across the country. You understand if you've been in one. The Ivanovs are in their sixties and do the room preparation and cleaning themselves. The motel guests are mostly truckers and power plant workers, and the Ivanovs work hard to keep their business successful. They never travel and work twenty-four seven. I don't envy their life.

Feodor walks out pulling a jacket on over his wrinkled shirt. He sees me and turns around to bring Sveta out. Feodor has a slightly balding head and a stomach girth to rival most. He likes his food.

It takes a few minutes before Sveta finally enters the lobby. Even sleepy, she smiles when she sees me. Her graying hair is pulled into a bun. I saw it loose once, and it fell to her waist. I like Sveta, and I quickly give her enough information to explain my needs. I then continue with, "I may lock the room and come back at some point. I'll leave an officer here to bar the door from anyone entering."

Sveta relays what I say to her husband. He nods his head as they speak to each other in Russian.

When they finish, I tell her, "I need to interview both of you, but right now I would like the names and personal information of guests from last night's occupied rooms." Sveta walks to her computer to pull the info I need. "How long have the Ledmens been here?" I ask while she's working. In most cases I would do this legwork, when and if I had probable cause. My problem is guests who can leave at any moment. Interviewing people over the phone is not good for courtroom testimony. I'm covering every base I can think of in case my findings suggest homicide.

"Months," Sveta replies without looking up from the screen. "He work at power plant," she says in her Russian flavored English.

It doesn't surprise me. Power plant employees travel around the country and often stay six months or more in one location.

I'm impatient to get inside the room and see what I'm facing. A few minutes later, I have a printed list of guests and their personal information minus credit card numbers. With paperwork in hand, I head back to the Ledmens' room. It's still dark out-side, and the double perimeter crime scene tape, which Leo put up, twirls silently in the shadows. Cars pass the motel in sparse inter-vals as they head toward the power plant and the early shift. My SUV doesn't have top lights and will go unnoticed. Leo's will be a problem.

Walking up to him, I circle my finger in the air. "Move your vehicle to the back so we can keep this low-key. I'm hoping people don't notice the tape when they drive past. It may give us a little longer before everyone and their brother comes over to see what's happening."

He nods and removes his key from his pocket. "Where do you want me stationed?"

"At the door. I need you to watch for guests leaving. Interview them if they can't wait for me. Basic information: Did they hear anything last night; has anything odd happened in the last week, etc. I'm treat-ing this as a full-on homicide until I know what I'm dealing with. I'm ready to go in-side." I place my hand out, and Leo hands me the motel room key. There's nothing fancy about the motel, and it doesn't have cards or fobs, simply good, old-fashioned keys with a green room tag displaying the number.

After moving to homicide, it took me six months to earn my advanced certification in DNA and evidence collection. It's a lot of work but waiting on a state forensic team is something we only do for large cases. Small to midsized police departments rely on cross-training for all employees, even civilians. The county sheriff's department has a civilian in charge of evidence. Sgt. Spence handles the evidence room at our department.

I take a few relaxing breaths and mentally review my checklist so far. I've covered everything I can think of. It's time to look inside the room.

Leo took my large evidence bag from Denise and placed it at the door of the motel room with my smaller bag before Mr. Ledmen was transferred to Denise's vehicle. I reach inside the larger of the two bags and pull out a plastic bag with hair covers, taking one out and tucking my hair inside. I pull a box of gloves out and carefully hook a finger inside the circle of the wrist, pulling it over my hand without getting DNA on the outside. Putting rubber gloves on for crime scenes is tedious. If you mess up, your DNA becomes mixed with that of others and makes the lab's processing harder. After getting the first pair of gloves on, I slide a second glove over each hand. This makes life easier in the long run.

After I'm partially in my gear, I direct my flashlight to the outside window and check for signs of forced entry. The metal holding the dirty glass is dusty, and there are no finger smudges visible. It doesn't appear the window's been opened in months. With the cold weather at this time of year, I'm not surprised.

After examining the glass, I place my flashlight back in my pocket, grab shoe covers, and put them over my sneakers. Next comes a facemask to keep my DNA from spraying around the room if I speak.

I turn to Leo. "I'm ready to go in. Keep the town back." I slowly enter the room. A lamp on a small table is the only illumination. Mrs. Ledmen is lying on the bed, on her side, with the covers pushed down to the foot of the bed. She's wearing a gray nightshirt and a pair of purple boxer shorts.

The first thing every detective wants to do is examine the body. I'm no different, but I know through training and experience that I need to look at the room first. I have no idea if Leo's suspicion was based on Mrs. Ledmen's body or other evidence. I take another deep breath through my nose and expel it slowly. The room is warmer than it is outside, but the body hasn't broken down enough to smell yet. I place my hands in my pockets to keep myself from accidently touching anything. This first exploration of the scene is only to observe.

Leo turns my way, watching me. If he were a rookie or unseasoned officer, I would have gone inside first and checked the scene before talking to Sveta at the front office. If Leo says something is suspicious, I'll take him at his word.

I glance around. The room is lived in. Boxes of food and other supplies lay stacked in the corner by the bed. A dresser is along the wall aligning with the door. Next to it is a clothing rack that isn't part of the hotel room and was either brought in by the Ledmens or left by another occupant. Normal items litter the top of the dresser such as a brush, water glass, and what looks like folded clean clothes. It matches with a couple occupying the room for an extended period. The small table in front of the window has two plates with half-eaten meals left behind, two glasses, and utensils.

There's a sink at the back of the room with more food containers stacked under the counter. A closet to the right side of the sink has the curtain pulled back with additional clothes inside. There is a small refrigerator next to the sink with a microwave on top and an electric hot plate on top of that. The refrigerator and microwave are part of the hotel amenities. The hot plate is not, but it's almost expected with a long-term stay. It's plugged into an outlet next to the sink along with an extension cord which leads into the dark bathroom. My eyes continue around the area and slide to the open bathroom door. I walk closer and remove my flashlight from my back pocket.

The first thing that catches my eye is a white toaster lying on its side on the floor. The cord isn't attached to the extension cord, but the plugs are close to each other. I examine the bathroom a little more closely. There's a wadded white towel in the far corner behind the toilet, opposite the bathtub. The room smells rather sour, and when I flash my light at the tub, I see black mildew on the shower curtain and wall.

It doesn't look like the room's been cleaned in a while. Sveta would at least clean the mold away if she came inside. My eyes are drawn back to the toaster which is all that's out of place. I squat low without letting my knees touch the floor and take a closer look.

When standing, I missed what Leo must have spotted to raise his suspicions. An approximate eight-inch pool of what looks like water is leaking from the inside of the toaster.

In detective training, we called this a clue.

Chapter Four

The Information Highway Opens

After looking through the bathroom again and seeing nothing else out of place, I backtrack to the body. Leo clears his throat from the door, and I look in his direction. "Yes, I saw the toaster. You should be a detective."

He cocks his head. "And go around with crap covering my gorgeous hair and face? No, thank you!"

We do our best not to laugh or even smile at a crime scene. I fight back a grin at his smart reply. Looks have never been a part of my job, but then again, I'm not an Italian man.

I begin looking closely at the victim. She's much smaller than her husband. She's lying on her side with her legs drawn partially to her chest. Her hands are curled and pulled in tight to her body. Mrs. Ledmen appears dry, but the bedding looks wet. I can't smell urine, but it would be unusual if her bladder hadn't released when she died. Once I roll the body, I'll be able to check for bladder and bowel leakage.

My eyes wander around the bed, but I don't see anything out of place. I decided to grab my camera and take the still photos I'll need. I glance over when Leo's phone rings.

"Yeah?" Leo is as articulate as I am in the morning. "No, Detective Jolett is here." A pause. "No, she's not requesting additional help."

It's not hard to figure out who's on the phone. Officer Stanley Conners is my nemesis; his father sits on the city council and is a thorn in the side of every cop at the department unless they're friends with Stanley. I am not.

"No," Leo continues. "We don't need traffic control; there's not a problem, but I'll call if Detective Jolett needs anything." Leo puts his phone back in his pocket, and I'm betting Stanley hung up on him.

So it begins.

Walking out of the room into the early morning darkness, I remove my shoe covers and my outer gloves, grabbing my camera from my SUV. The next part of the job is long and tedious.

I grab the photo log out of the large evidence bag and hand it to Leo. "I'll give you the picture number and tell you what I'm shooting. Slow me down or correct me if I make a mistake. You'll need to stay at the door so you can see if anyone approaches." I don't mention Stanley because we both know I'm now working on borrowed time as far as having no interruptions. Stanley's father will call the police chief, and the chief will call me.

I walk outside the outer crime scene tape and begin taking pictures of the parking lot and the front of the motel room while softly calling out what I'm shooting. I walk up to each vehicle in the parking lot and snap pictures of the entire car followed by the license plates. I slowly move in closer to the room and take a picture of the door so it includes the room number. "Number thirty-one, outside motel room door," I call. "Number thirty-two, looking into the motel room door."

Before I enter the room, I place another pair of gloves over the single pair I left on. I then take out two more foot covers for my feet.

I take one hundred and sixty-two still shots of the room and body before I go back to the doorway. I don't step out this time because I don't want to put on new gloves and booties.

"Call Brett and get him out of bed. I want him holding people back. I need you inside with me." Brett is our part-time animal control officer. He's moody and prefers animals over people. He's stood guard for me on scenes before, and the best thing about him is he isn't married and, as far as I've known, doesn't share inside police information with anyone.

Leo makes the call, and I turn my camera setting to video. I pan the room completely then walk slowly inside to capture video of the entire scene. Before I finish, the sound of Brett's diesel animal control engine rumbles outside the room. The sun is just rising over the horizon. A convenience store is directly across the street, and I notice two people pointing in our direction.

"Tell Brett to park his vehicle parallel to the front door and block the room from view. I don't want anyone seeing the body."

"Yes, ma'am." Leo says just to be smart. It's his Italian heritage. Like Tony, my old partner who was also Italian, Leo can't help himself. I miss Tony so much. He never put up with my crap. Losing Tony started my dark days until Suii gave me hope. Now my partnership is all on Bell. I glance at my SUV and know I'll need to give her a break soon. She'll wait for hours if needed, but I don't like it.

Leo and Brett approach after Brett's car is situated.

"Hi, Brett. Thanks for coming. I need you to hold the scene."

"No problem." Brett turns his back on us. As I said, he's not much of a people person, and he never seems to have questions.

I turn to Leo. "Too bad I need to ruin those good looks. Glove, hair, mask, and bootie up so you're as good-looking as me."

"You know if someone sees me, it'll ruin my rep."

"I'll be sure to take a pic and send it to the local newspaper." I roll my eyes. "I'll be taking pictures inside drawers, cabinets, and the refrigerator before we tackle the body."

"You've got to be kidding me," Leo mutters.

"Nope. If I have an unsolved crime here, another detective will look at the case file years from now and thank me. Hurry up and let's get to work."

Once he's inside, looking like my twin, I begin my next set of pictures. I open each drawer, snap a shot, and move on. Leo fills out the photo log and manages to avoid groaning.

After taking the first set of photographs, it's time to examine the body. I inspect what I can see before taking pictures. After the next set of photographs, I examine the body a little more closely. Leo then helps me roll Mrs. Ledmen over. The only way I can help him is to find leverage by placing my knees on the bed. Something wet soaks into my jeans where the right one touched the bed closest to the body. This is not the time to think about what it is. It will be hours before I have time to change. I pull the body toward me, and Leo pushes in my direction. Once we have Mrs. Ledmen on her back and her stiff hands sticking up, I can see her curled fingers clearly.

There's a severe burn on the fingers of her right hand which is curled inward. I can't make out the entire burn area, but it's sizable. I'll admit I'm not familiar with electrocution and as far as I know we've never had a case at the department.

Leo's eyes go large above his mask when he sees what is holding my attention.

I literally can't help myself and say what I'm thinking aloud. "Death by toaster."

Leo's eyes go larger, and he looks back down at the burn. "You said I was second on this one."

I nod.

"Good. This case interests me," he says. "If you need help after my initial report, just let me know."

Before I answer, my cell rings. The word

"Chief" shows on my caller ID, and I show it to Leo. I get off the bed and walk to the door while peeling my outer gloves off each hand. Again, I don't step outside but chuck the used gloves out the door and remove my mask to answer. The last thing I want is dead body gunk on my phone, especially when the phone goes near my mouth.

"Good morning, sir. I'm glad you called," I say honestly. I like the chief. I also know he's calling because of Stanley's father and not my earlier message.

The chief dives in. "Councilman Conners just left my house. Thank you for the heads-up waiting for me. I had Conners sit down and then excused myself for the bathroom to check my phone."

The fact Conners went to the chief's house means Stanley couldn't get inside information. "What did you tell him?" I ask calmly.

"I told him that my detective was on-scene and she had everything under control. He wants an update in two hours, and I told him I would not discuss an open investigation. I wouldn't be surprised if he shows up at your scene and tries to bully his way in. Arrest his ass if that happens. Who do you have with you?"

I catch him up on Leo, Denise, and Brett helping me along with what I have so far, in the beginning stages of my case. He listens silently and offers no advice because I know my job. A minute later, we end our call, and I beckon Leo over.

I wave to get Brett's attention, and he walks over to the door. "Let me know immediately if Officer or Councilman Conners shows up. They're not allowed on my scene, and I will personally take care of them if they try. The two of you need to stay out of this; they already dislike me."

Brett's expression doesn't change. "No sweat off my back; if you say they can't come in, I'm not letting them in."

"Thanks, Brett, that's why I called you in on this one. Add the time you're here to your weekly hours, no flexing out. The chief will see you get paid."

He gives a nod and walks back to his post.

"I'm not afraid of the Conners. The old

man didn't like when I went on the drug task force and his son wasn't selected. Funny that when I came out of the task force, he wasn't selected again."

I give Leo a level stare. "You're both taking all the fun out of my day. I really wanted to arrest the councilman."

"If we get the chance, we can flip for it."

With our agreement made, I slip my mask back up and add another pair of gloves. I also grab clear packaging tape and two brown lunch bags from my evidence bag. I walked over to the bed and slip the bags over Mrs. Ledmen's hands, taping them securely at the wrists. As I continue examining her body, I notice bruises on her legs and a small one on the side of her chest. I only see it because her shirt was partially pulled up. The medical examiner will remove her clothes, and I'll be able to see her entire body. Hopefully, it will give me more answers.

My eyes continue their journey while Leo stands next to the bed, watching. She's wearing socks, and blood oozes from a wound on the top of her foot. It looks fairly

SUZIE IVY

large, and I'll have a closer inspection at the autopsy.

Stepping away, I notice the knee of my jeans has a defined wet spot and the bed appears wet around her lower midsection. When I look up, Leo is staring at my knee.

"This is exactly why I'd rather be a traffic cop," he says.

I shake my head. "You've handled plenty of bodies at traffic scenes."

He scratches his arm with his glove and then realizes what he did. "Those bodies don't pee on me."

He's pushing it. "Be sure to wash that uniform before wearing it again."

His face goes white, and he looks down at his arms where he touched it with the glove. "I'll do that."

Chapter Five

Gathering Evidence

The sun is making a full appearance when Brett calls from outside the door. "There's a man from the room next door packing up his vehicle."

"Stall him for a few. I'll be right out."

Leo stays with Mrs. Ledmen while I divest myself of all my protective gear and hustle outside. I rummage through my small evidence bag and find the backup recorder I carry. I hit the switch and no little green light shows so I rummage some more and find the double A batteries I need. After switching out the batteries, I'm set.

Brett gives a chin nod to the door on the west side of the Ledmen room. Before I knock, a man walks out with a small bag slung over his shoulder and heads to his car without noticing me. I approach while he's stowing his bag behind the driver's seat.

"Hi, I'm Detective Jolett. I need to speak with you for a moment." The man appears to be in his fifties, short, graying hair, and an easy smile.

"Sure, Detective, what's going on?"

"We've had a problem in the room next to yours, and I have a few questions."

He looks to the door before glancing back at me. "Is she seriously hurt?"

His response opens a new door of questions. "Can you tell me why you think she would be hurt?"

He runs his fingers through his hair. People are funny. They want to help, but our world is also one of "no involvement" and people must decide for themselves. As a witness to a possible homicide, I could take this man to the station for questioning. I'd rather him decide he wants to help and freely give me what he knows.

I see the decision in his eyes before he speaks. "I came in yesterday at about three in the afternoon. I have a ten-hour drive to get home and wanted to drive straight through but knew I wouldn't make it."

He glances around again, and I wait. People will always fill the silence if you give them a chance.

"I heard a man and woman arguing at around six yesterday evening. I almost asked to have my room changed, but things went quiet and I didn't hear anything again until around nine."

"When you heard them arguing, could you make out what they were saying?"

"A woman was crying and yelling a lot, but I didn't hear what she said until she yelled, 'Stop, you're hurting me.'" He runs his fingers through his hair again. "I should have done something."

I can't answer that for him. "What happened at nine?"

He shakes his head a bit. "Just a thump against the wall."

"How long do you think they were arguing earlier in the evening when the woman yelled out?

"Maybe ten minutes."

I quickly fire my next question. "Did you ever physically see either of the people in the room next door?

He rests back on his car door a bit. "No, I heard the door open and close a few times and the ice maker go off but that was earlier. After the argument, the next thing I heard was the thump against the wall, then nothing."

"Could you make out what the argument was about?"

"I never understood what the man was saying." He pauses for a moment. "Is she dead?"

I can't answer that truthfully. If he eats breakfast in town and tells a waiter, it will be a huge hassle. "No. I need your driver's license information to add to my report and a phone number if I have more questions."

People's memories work in strange ways. He'll drive home, and something will pop into his head he wishes he mentioned. I take his license information and scribble his phone number in the small notepad I carry. I hand him my card which has my office number on it.

"If you think of anything else, please call me."

"May I leave?"

"Yes, drive safely. I'll call if I think of any more questions, and I really appreciate your help." I shake his hand before he climbs behind the wheel and drives away.

"Thanks, Brett," I say after the interview. He nods and I walk to my SUV and pop the back. "Down, stay." I command Bell and give her a gentle pat on the head." She looks at Brett and gives a small whine. He's one of the humans she likes. "Go ahead, you can say hi." When working, I give Bell one-word commands so there's never confusion. She understands full sentences, though and I'm always amazed at her brain capacity. With a six-foot leap from the back of the car, she pounces to Brett's side. He goes to a knee and gives her proper attention.

"What a pretty girl you are. So beautiful," he praises.

Brett wasn't around when I had Suii. Our city council approves a different budget from year to year and sometimes there's money for part-time animal control and sometimes not. The local animal shelter takes on more responsibility along with our patrol officers when the position is not budgeted. The department runs better when Brett handles the animal calls.

After proper attention, Bell gives a small bark and looks around. Brett steps back, and I attach her leash to the strap at the back of her neck. "Time to do your business, and then it's more time in the hatch for slumber. I promise we'll have an extra-long playdate later." I lead her to a small patch of grass.

Bell sniffs around and inspects a few of good spots like any good detective before choosing the perfect one to squat on. I've asked her about this process several times, but she's decided not to share. I won't give up, and maybe someday, she'll let me in on the trick. At least this time there's nothing to pick up when she's done, and we're both happy. I give her a generous scratch at the scruff of her neck and let her know I love her. Bell doesn't complain when I put her back in the SUV. She understands her job is to rest and be ready for whatever comes.

I quickly gear up and grab a pack of sticky notes along with a black Sharpie. I sling my camera over my shoulder and enter the room again.

"Did you have an interesting conversation with Mrs. Ledmen and solve my case?" I ask with a straight face. Leo is standing at the front window looking out.

"You're funny," he says and looks over. "I know it will make your job harder, but she hasn't uttered a word."

"Too bad, I could use some answers," I say as I walk to the bathroom. Something started bugging me while Bell did her business, and I need to check it out. I enter the bathroom and look in the shower at the porcelain and also the wall. I stretch the shower curtain out and examine the folds.

Nothing is wet.

I glance back down at the toaster. Nothing has changed, and the water is still pooled next to it.

If you were going to electrocute yourself or someone else with a toaster, you would need water. The tub is dry. I step out and look into the sink outside the bathroom. Dry. Taking another step inside the bathroom door, my eye travels to the only other source of water in the room. It's sitting in the toilet. I have even more questions now.

I don't say anything to Leo. It's time to collect evidence. I stride past him and grab swabs and swab boxes from my small evidence bag. I hand Leo my camera as I walk past him. "Change gloves so you don't get goop on my equipment and grab the evidence log from my small bag before you join me."

"Yes, ma'am." He salutes without touching his face. I ignore his quip and head back into the bathroom.

With the Sharpie, I begin numbering the sticky notes. Number 1 is placed on the floor by the water. Number 2, on the toaster, number 3, the seat next to the rim of the bowl and so on. The shower and curtain are also tagged. We have yellow plastic tent shaped numbers for outside work, but I prefer my paper stickies when inside.

I turn to Leo. "I need a close-up of each tagged item." He grumbles good-naturedly before doing what I say. I step back and let him take the pictures.

He lowers the camera and turns to me. "Why are you tagging the shower, curtain, and toilet?"

"I want to know where the water came from. The shower is dry, so I'll add a little saline and swab it. There's a little dampness on an inside crease of the curtain so I'll get that too. My guess is the water came from the toilet."

His eyes above his mask light up. "You're kidding me?"

I shrug. "I wish." I don't have time to discuss my thoughts at this point. "I need to grab my saline ampules. I'll be right back."

I walk to the front door and check outside.

Brett gives a chin nod in the direction of the small store across the street. "A few people lined up and are trying to see inside the room." He's standing at the back of his vehicle with his arms crossed. Brett might be a softy when it comes to animals, but people are different and he's intimidating.

"Keep doing what you're doing. I'll shut the door and leave you to it." I almost remind him to keep people behind the crime scene tape but manage to stop myself. Brett knows what I need.

I locate the ampules, close the front door, and walk back to the bathroom. I form the swab boxes by pushing in the right areas so they form a tube and number them to correspond with my sticky tags. Leo holds the boxes for me while I remove a swab package from my pocket. The swab sticks are about five inches long with two to a pack. I use both to get my first sample of clear fluid from inside the toaster, calling out the number and description. Leo checks his watch and writes down the time for each item collected. He hands me the boxes as I need them. It takes another thirty minutes to get my samples before I collect evidence from the rest of the room. It takes another hour to get what I need. When I'm finished, I make the call to have Mrs. Ledmen's body picked up by the coroner. It's time to speak with Mr. Ledmen.

Chapter Six

Questions Questions Questions

It's eight in the morning when I head into the station to question Mr. Ledmen. I spoke with Denise an hour before, and she said he was quiet and not making waves. She also mentioned he's cried a few times. Leo heads home to sleep. Poor man has been out all night. At least I slept until three.

While Bell does her business, we have a short chat. "This is a strange one, Bell. If you have any ideas, toss them my way like a good partner, will you?" She keeps her thoughts to herself but has no problem sharing slobber. I wipe it off on her fur and give her head a quick pat. Her large brown eyes peer up at mine, and my heart squeezes a bit. "Let's go inside and solve this case."

I enter the department through the

squad room so I can set up the interview room before speaking with Mr. Ledmen. I put Bell in my office and give her a chew bone before I remove the evidence from my car and place it in two evidence lockers so I can show the chain of custody without showing a prolonged time sitting in my vehicle. I mark the time everything is carried inside before heading to the interview room.

The room is small with a table and two chairs and a shelf in the back. We keep the breathalyzer machine on the shelf, and the patrol guys use it when they have a possible drunk driver. The video evidence is sometimes more powerful than the actual breath alcohol content. Back in my patrol days, I had drunks slide off the chair, land on their butt, and look up at me like, what just happened. Those cases are always easier to prosecute in court.

Video is vital as a detective too. Sometimes I'll miss an expression or even a comment the person I'm interviewing makes. After rewatching interview videos, I catch the small stuff, and many of my cases have been solved this way.

I pick up a wadded tissue left behind by one of the officers and toss it into the garbage, giving one last look at the room before I'm satisfied it's ready. I take Mr. Ledmen's phone from my pocket and remove it from a plastic bag. I place it on the table where I want Mr. Ledmen sitting. I walk into my office and check the green light on the camera recording equipment. It's set.

It's time for our interview.

When I enter the front records office, Mr. Ledmen is sitting on the couch, and Denise is in the chair next to him. Mr. Ledmen is flipping through a magazine, and Denise is flipping through her phone. Youth.

"Hi, Mr. Ledmen, I'm sorry it took me so long to get here. I stayed until your wife was removed." This isn't a lie. "I have a few questions before you leave."

"Where is my wife?" he asks first.

"She's at the mortuary." This is also true, but she's in a special room, locked in a refrigerator, awaiting the trip to the medical examiner's office.

"My phone. I need to call my son."

My heart drops. "How old is your son?" I ask gently.

"He's nineteen. He's actually my stepson, but I've been his dad for seventeen years so to me, he's my son."

"Your cell is in the interview room. If you could give me just a bit longer before calling him so I can ask my questions, I will get you out of here sooner." Unless Mr. Ledmen admits he killed his wife, he's walking out today. I won't have the evidence I need to arrest until after the autopsy, and that's if the autopsy shows electrocution as cause of death. There's also the possibility Mrs. Ledmen tried to kill herself by placing a toaster in the toilet. At this point, I have no idea what I really have so this interview is important.

"I need to call my boss too," Mr. Ledmen says. "I'm sure he's been calling my phone nonstop. I never miss work, and I've never been late."

I really don't want him making calls first, and I need to be careful at this point. I need him volunteering information and not feeling like he's being forced to answer my questions. "Follow me. We won't be long but bring your water if you'd like."

We enter the interview room, and I take the chair at the back, leaving him to take the chair where his phone sits. He clicks on the screen, and it lights up with messages. I had already looked at them before I bagged the phone. I could only see what displayed on the screen, and they were all from his boss. Mrs. Ledmen's phone is in evidence, and I'm hoping he doesn't ask for it right away.

"If you could give me a few minutes for questions, I have no problem with you making calls in here."

He puts the phone down. "Sure." His voice sounds resigned.

He's free to leave at any time so I don't read him his Miranda rights. I need a baseline story to begin the legwork of this investigation. I look at him. "It might be easier if you start from yesterday and walk me through the entire day."

He looks down at his fingers which are linked together in front of him. "I went to work at six and came home at six thirty." He glances up. "Mary had dinner ready, but she wasn't in a good mood and started in on me as soon as I walked through the door. She was also drinking. She hates it here and says there's nothing for her to do all day. I warned her of this when she insisted on coming." He stops talking and looks up like a memory has popped into his head. He doesn't share it. "We argued, and she stopped drinking around eight when she took her sleep medication."

I had packaged her meds. She was taking anti-depressant and anti-anxiety medications along with a few others I wasn't familiar with.

"What happened after that?"

His red eyes close for a moment, and he speaks when they open. "She went into the bathroom, and I fell asleep. I woke up because I heard something, and she was passed out in front of the sink." He exhales, and his shoulders slump. "I dragged her onto the bed. I think she hit the side wall with her hip or leg." Again, he goes quiet. "I know this looks bad. We were fighting, and I feel terrible. I wasn't gentle when I dragged her onto the bed. I was angry she passed out again. This looks bad, doesn't it?" he repeats.

So far, what he's told me matches the crime scene. Dragging her onto the bed while she was still alive matched the bruises on her body. They wouldn't be there if he dragged her after death. This doesn't mean they didn't happen in an entirely different way too. Time will tell.

"Did you see the toaster on the bathroom floor?" I throw out. I want his physical response as well as his verbal.

His head jerks slightly, but he looks me in the eye when he responds. "I saw it on the floor. It wasn't plugged in."

"Have you ever physically hurt your wife?"

He shakes his head while answering. "No, if you mean hit her or anything like that. When she's drunk, she hits me sometimes, but it never hurts." He looks down. "I guess that doesn't matter anymore."

"Did you report when she hit you?"

Again, he shakes his head. "She never hurt me. She just pushes me away or slaps my arm." Tears begin running down his cheeks. "I didn't hurt my wife last night. I may have bumped her against the wall when I carried her to bed, but it wasn't intentional."

"Thank you." I give him a soft smile and push a box of tissue closer. "I'm truly sorry for your loss, Mr. Ledmen. Your room at the motel won't be available for a few hours or possibly tomorrow." I needed to get an electrician in before I release the room. I keep this to myself. "I know you probably need your things, and I promise to let you into the room as soon as possible."

"May I leave?"

"Absolutely. Give me your cell number so I can call you as soon as I release the room."

"Sure." He reads off the number, and I write it down. "What about her body? We live in Texas, and she would want to be buried there." His voice hitches.

"I don't know why your wife died, and I've ordered an autopsy." Mr. Ledmen has the usual response when faced with someone you love being cut up after death, and I see the grimace in his eyes and expression. "I will be with her during the autopsy. I know you don't know me, but I have compassion for you and your wife. My job at this point is to also keep your wife safe and that includes her body."

"Thank you."

"I'll know more by the end of the day. Would you like to make your phone calls in here before you leave? I can have Denise drop you wherever you'd like. A hotel if you want."

"No, thanks. I have a friend who can pick me up. I usually stay with him when we're here, but I got the room because of my wife. I don't want to go back to Texas without her body."

"I completely understand." I stand up and head to the door. "Make your calls and then you can wait in the front office for your friend. Just come out when you're ready; we won't disturb you."

I walk out, head to Denise, and give her a finger beckon to follow me into my office. She walks in and eyes Bell closely, staying as far from her as possible.

"Bell, stay." I give her a hand command too then pull two chairs from in front of the video monitor. "Mr. Ledmen is making his calls, and this way I can hear what he says. Ignore Bell and she'll ignore you." The entire department knows Bell, and they know exactly what she's capable of. I see Denise's nervousness and I understand. It's one thing to have me controlling Bell's leash and another for her to have the freedom to attack. I know my dog, and I trust her to do as I command.

Denise finally tears her eyes away. "Does Mr. Ledmen know you're recording him?"

"He didn't ask, and I didn't volunteer the information."

He's on the phone with his son when I turn up the volume. He cries through much of the phone call and keeps repeating, "I'm sorry, son. I'm sorry." After about five painful minutes, he hangs up and calls his boss only to break down again. Last, he calls his friend. He stops crying before his friend answers and then manages to hold it together while telling his friend Mary died. He requests a place to stay and a pickup from the police department. In all, he spends about ten minutes making calls.

"You're going to let him leave."

To be a rookie again. "I have no choice. I don't have evidence of a crime, and I need help with a few things before I can determine what happened. I'm treating this as a homicide until I have proof it isn't. Remember to keep what you've seen and heard today quiet."

"Got it. If you no longer need me, I have reports to write."

"That works. I'll let you know if I need help with something. I know staying with Mr. Ledmen wasn't fun, but it helped me a lot."

"He was okay. Just sad."

I can see being sad if your wife dies. I can also see being sad that you killed her in the heat of the moment. If this was planned, I can see being sad that law enforcement is involved. There are many reasons people act as they do. The problem is discovering what they are.

Chapter Seven

Lessons in Electricity

I feed Bell from her stash in my office and grab a protein bar after bringing my emergency bag in from my car. Bell comes with me into the evidence room while I process everything. The door is closed, and no one can hear us. Bell is my partner in more ways than protection and explosives. She listens to me talk through my cases and allows my brain to come up with answers. It's become our thing.

"Everything points to her being killed by the toaster. Her bruises could be from hitting the wall at any time before death." Bell finishes her food, walks over, and plops herself on her blanket. She has a kennel here, but we rarely use it. "I need to look up information on the internet. I've heard of death by toaster but never really considered it a thing." Bell yawns, not helping my analysis in the least. "You lay there and contemplate what I've told you while I call the county attorney's office and run the case past Sam." Bell rolls over and closes her eyes.

Samantha Anderson is the assistant county attorney and handles felony cases. She's married with children, and I've often wondered how she holds it together playing mommy after some of my cases come across her desk. I call her cell, and she picks up on the third ring.

"I have a strange one to run past you."

"Shoot." This is county attorney humor.

I explain everything that's happened to this point and finish with, "Bell is fresh out of ideas. I need an electrician, and she doesn't know of any."

I receive a chuckle. "My brother's an electrician. I'll call him and have him send over someone he trusts. I don't want my brother working the case and causing a problem because we're related."

She answered my question before I asked. She's right. Having family work on a possible homicide case wouldn't look good.

"Can you think of anything I've missed?" I ask after we talk a bit more.

"Not at this point. Death by toaster will make a huge splash in the newspaper."

She's right. "I'll do my best to keep it from the paper. Councilman Conners has already called the chief."

"Figures. Have fun with that."

"Always."

We disconnect, and I look at Bell whose ears perk up. "I say we get in a little K9 work after I call the medical examiner to set up the autopsy."

As I said, Bell understands quite a bit, and she knows she won't be waiting patiently much longer. Her thumping tail tells me so. When Suii came into my life, I didn't need to contend with a tail. His was cropped. Bell on the other hand waves hers around, knocking things over every chance she gets. It took a few days before I realized it was easier to move the water glass I keep on my living room coffee table to the center of the table so it wasn't susceptible to her tail. All partners come with problems. Bell's is twelve inches long.

I make an appointment for the autopsy the next afternoon. As soon as I hang up, Samantha calls me back and says an electrician will meet me at the motel in two hours. It's enough time to get in a good set with Bell.

I leave her in my office and hit the evidence room again. There's a special locker where I store small amounts of explosive to use for Bell's training. I grab a small baggy and start hiding items in strategic places in the squad room.

"I'm bringing Bell through so I can mark some training in her journal. Stay where you're at and you'll be fine."

Denise gives me a slight smile. She isn't comfortable around Bell, and maybe someday that will change. Bell hasn't gone out of her way to make friends, but that's Bell. She took to Brett easily and Leo after a few months. She also took to my next-door neighbor's dog, Sugarplum. Bell hasn't given Ed, the neighbor, the time of day, but she loves Sugarplum.

Suii and Sugarplum got along too. At least they did after I told Suii to eat the little yapper. It took a while, but we finally came around and friended Ed. I wasn't the nicest person back in the day, but Ed never threw my bad behavior back at me. He was devastated when Suii died. It's nice to have a neighbor to watch my place while I'm at work, and Ed takes the job seriously.

I continue placing items around the squad room until the small baggy is empty. I can only do this at the department on weekends and evenings. Otherwise, the building is too crowded. I also have a few abandoned places in town that work for training, and every once in a while, I use the inside of the schools. It helps me know my way around in case we have a bomb threat.

After attaching Bell's leash, I tell her it's time to work. Her entire body does an excited shake. She's always excited to work. I lead her to the squad room and start at one end. When Bell smells what she's trained to detect, she puts her nose down and barks. Canines are trained differently. With her cross-training, she's ready at every step to attack.

"Stay. Guard," I say. She turns her butt to

the small blasting cap hidden in the corner, looks around the room and growls.

"Good girl. Release." She wags her tail while I mark her success in my book. We continue until she's found all the items I hid.

"You're a good girl; let's play." She jumps up, twists, and whines. "I know," I tell her. "Let's grab your toy." Her toy is a thick rope in my office, and it's her favorite. I have one just like it at home and another in the back of my car. They are identical with large orange and purple stripes. The toy means she did her job, and it's time for her reward. We head outside to roughhouse behind the department in a gated lunch area that's empty on the weekends. I release Bell's leash and toss the rope. She attacks, growls while shaking it in her mouth, and acts like it's something she's never seen before. She tosses it up, catches it, and does it again. I give her a few minutes before calling her over, taking the rope from her mouth and throwing it again.

When I partnered with Suii, I didn't like dogs. Now Bell is my life just as Suii was. I'm a different person. The anger I felt at the death of my partner, Tony, is gone. A sad ache is there, and I doubt it will ever leave. Tony was special, and he would have loved Bell and Suii. I know he would be happy that I finally have something to make me smile again, and Bell does that daily.

I allow her to play for thirty minutes before bringing her water. After she's made a mess around the water bowl, I load her back into my SUV. I clear the station and head to the motel where Brett is standing guard.

"If you can stay for a bit longer, it would really help," I tell Brett. "I'm meeting someone in a few minutes. After he goes through, I should be able to release the room."

"You got it."

Before he finishes his short sentence, I notice a van with Daily Electric plastered on the side pulling up beside Brett's animal control vehicle. I wave him over once he turns off the engine.

Introductions are made. The electrician gives his name as Malcom. I explain that Brett will remain outside to keep people back, and I take him inside. Mrs. Ledmen's body is no longer here, and the wet spot on the bed has thankfully dried. The less Malcom knows, the less he can spread around town. "I actually understand nothing about electricity and need to know if it's possible to tell if someone was electrocuted by checking the wiring." Malcom is at least sixty with shaggy gray hair, a just-as-shaggy gray beard, and stark blue eyes that sparkle even through a face of hair.

"Circuit would blow."

"Okay. Can you check the circuits?"

"Yep. Any specific circuit you want me checking?"

"All of them?" I ask in question.

"Yep." He sets his toolbox on the carpet and heads to the receptacle beneath the front window. He looks at it then goes to the next receptacle.

"I need to know if any are blown and how many if they are."

"No safety circuit. It's usually in the bathroom, but some rooms have more than one, and I want to be sure." He checks each receptacle before heading into the bathroom. He points to the one next to the sink. "It's a GFCI outlet, and it's blown."

"What does that mean?" I ask. He pulls a screwdriver from his pocket and begins unscrewing the plate. "Shouldn't you turn off the power?"

I receive a grunt for asking a stupid question to an electrician. When he pulls the plate away, black coats the inside. Malcom sticks his finger to the exposed wires and brings it out. Holding his finger toward me, he says, "Someone had quite the party with this."

"How would it happen?"

"Too much for the circuit to handle." He looks around. "Multiple extension cords, faulty extension cord, or even faulty appliance. Sometimes a circuit just runs its course and needs to be changed out."

I couldn't ask the one question burning a hole in my head. "Could a toaster in the toilet do this?" Nope. I couldn't ask that. So I ask, "Is this the only blown circuit in the room?"

"I think so, but I'll remove all the plates and double-check to see if there's damage to any other outlets."

It takes him about thirty minutes. The other outlets have no damage. Once he's gone, I review what I learned. The outlet next to the sink has a blown circuit. Thankfully, if this goes to trial, Malcom will be called in to explain the outlets and circuits, and I'll learn only what's needed to understand death by electricity. Watching Malcom stick a screwdriver to each outlet with electricity running was not my idea of fun. I also know I don't want to have his job.

Brett helps me remove the crime scene tape then takes off. I return the room key to Sveta and Feodor. Sveta translates, and they both answer a few questions. They noticed nothing strange about the couple, and Sveta says Mrs. Ledmen was nice.

"You can rent the room out, but the bed will need to be replaced. The body leaked on it, and there's no telling what it was. I promise it wasn't good."

Sveta grimaces slightly and gives me a small smile. "Thank you," she says politely.

I leave the office and call the chief. He answers which surprises me. "Councilman Conners has called three times," he says in annoyance.

"This is an active investigation. You

would think he would understand that by now."

The chief's chuckle sounds over the line. "I'll deal with the councilman. I just wanted you to know he's a dog with a bone and won't be giving up."

"My crew has strict instructions to keep their mouths shut. The only other person at the department I'll be talking to is Detective Macky."

"It will get out sooner or later."

"I have a lot of groundwork to do so I need it to be later." I don't envy the chief's need to keep the city council happy. They hire and fire the chief of police and see their position as one of authority over our department. It isn't. They have no more rights than the public to know information about an open investigation. It puts the chief between a rock and a hard place. He does his job; I do mine.

"Understood," he says. "Sergeant Spence will be back in town on Wednesday. Report your findings to him, and I'll be out of it." If only it were that easy. I know the chief will have up-to-the-minute reports directly from the sergeant once he's back.

"I'm heading home to sleep. The autopsy is first thing in the morning. I'll let Detective Macky know." Macky would take detective calls while I'm at the autopsy which was a few hours away.

"Good job so far, Jolett."

We ended our call. I was a huge pain in the ass to the department for a long time. Anger and sadness kept me from healing after Tony's death. My sergeant and the chief put up with a lot, and I didn't know if I would ever be in the chief's good graces again.

"Hear that, Bell? So far, I've done a good job. The fact I'm investigating this by the skin of my teeth should tell you something." I wait for Bell to respond but like usual, she doesn't. "It should tell you that even with a possible death by toaster, you want Detective Jolett on your case."

I don't receive a bark or growl in reply. I guess Bell agrees.

Chapter Eight

Fly Zapper

The following morning, after tossing and turning all night, I leave Bell behind when I leave for the medical examiner's office. If I take her, the engine will need to run while I'm at the autopsy, and I have no idea how long I'll be. I called Ed last night. He has a key, and if he hears anything strange, he'll check on her. Bell has a dog door, which I had installed after she was trapped inside once for twelve hours. She won't go to the bathroom on the carpet, and I felt really guilty she suffered so long. The pet door was my way of apologizing, and Bell accepted it after she decided the rubber flapper in the door wasn't a personal afront to her ego when it slaps her in the butt. If I'm home, she won't use it. I think she laughs when I open and close the door for her so many times a day. She wants to know how well I stay trained.

Right now, she follows me around as I get ready, whining softly as her way of letting me know she isn't happy about being left behind.

"I'm sorry you can't go. You would be bored the entire time," I tell her sincerely. She gives me puppy-dog eyes and huffs as she plops down at my feet. "I'll take you hiking next weekend," I promise. Her tail thumps up and down exactly twice. She's saying she'll believe it when she sees it and next weekend is a long time from now.

I give her a favored treat before walking out the door a little early. It's Sunday and traffic should be light, but you never know. I review everything I have for the hundredth time during the ride. Hopefully, the autopsy will hold answers.

The medical examiner's office is next to the trauma center in the city. I have bodies shipped here because it's the best in the state.

Dr. Thomas is the ME on duty. The lab operates seven days a week around the clock. I've never had to wait more than

SUZIE IVY

forty-eight hours for an autopsy.

"Hi, Detective Jolett. Your name popped up on the screen this morning so I'm hoping it's something good."

He means interesting. I've had a string of interesting cases in my career, and I won't be disappointing him today. "Death by toaster."

He looks startled for a moment and then chuckles. Before going to sleep the night before, I Googled "death by toaster." There were more than ten thousand results. The best information I could find was an average of fifty people die a year in the US from electrocution. Of those, one died from a small appliance last year. It didn't say what the appliance was, and I could find no other information.

"You laugh but Google it. I dare you," I snap back in challenge.

His smile disappears, and I can see the weariness in his eyes. "Come into my office and tell me about your case."

I do just that without mentioning the burns on Mrs. Ledmen's hand and possibly her foot. As I speak, his slight grin appears. "You actually think a toaster killed this woman?" he finally asks me.

"I'm hoping, if she was murdered, it was her husband and not the toaster. It won't be easy to prosecute otherwise."

"You're killing me," he says on a half laugh, half groan. "Gear up and let's see what you have." We leave the office with me trailing slightly behind. He uses his fingerprint on a small box outside the autopsy area and pushes through the door when the light on the box goes from red to green. He leaves me in a small room where I can gown up. I put on a mask, gloves, and eye protection before walking out. One of the assistants wheels the cart with Mrs. Ledmen into a large cubicle just as Dr. Thomas approaches. I have my camera ready and so does his assistant. The ME's office will send me their pictures, but I hate waiting and learned to take my own. Dr. Thomas starts at Mrs. Ledmen's head and examines her eyes. He quickly moves to her arms. He pulls the left one out straight before moving to the right. Speaking into his recorder, he comments on the burn to the back of her fingers but doesn't look at me.

Slowly, Dr. Thomas moves to her feet which are now bare. He stops when he sees the burn on her foot. He looks up at me and shakes his head. "You may have a death by toaster."

I don't so much as smile. This headline won't be good.

The giant fly zapper located in the corner of the room sparks, and I jump at least two inches. I hate that thing. Dr. Thomas and his assistant laugh at me. Everyone but those working here jumps when the zapper goes off. I may not like the thing, but I dislike maggots more.

It's an hour before I'm on the road. The blood draw for toxicology will take a week to ten days for results to come back, depending on how busy the lab is. Besides the burns on Mrs. Ledmen's hand and foot, the autopsy didn't show anything more than the bruises on her chest and legs that I'd already discovered. Samples of her heart, liver, and kidneys will also go to the lab. Dr. Thomas knew enough about electrical shock to explain there might be proof in her blood and muscle tissue due to seizure and muscle constriction. It isn't much, and the chances are good that Mr. Ledmen will leave town if I need to wait two weeks for evidence from the autopsy. It's what I'm left with, though.

I head straight to the station and run into Detective Macky. "Jolett," he says with a smile. "The rumor mill is saying you have a live one."

"Oh, really. They're speculating or someone has loose lips and will lose their job?"

He smiles. "I've got your back, tiger. Officer Conners is running his mouth. He tried hitting me up for info, and I didn't even need to lie."

That gets a smile out of me. "Let's go into my office, and I'll give you what I have. I need another pair of eyes on this. Bell is coming up short."

"Bell is the best detective I know. I think she needs a new partner."

"Fill out the paperwork and someone might take pity on you." It was nice to joke at work again. I'm glad Gabe forgave me for the jerk I was post-Suii.

"If you're willing to give me lessons in disgruntlement, I might get a K9."

I ignore his prod. We both take a seat at my desk, me behind and Gabe in front. I tear the entire case down for him, including Dr. Thomas' thoughts which weren't much.

My office phone rings, and I hold a finger up to Gabe before picking up the receiver. "Detective Jolett speaking."

"Dispatch. We have a man on the line who would like to speak to you about his deceased mother."

I give Gabe a thumbs-up. "Put him through, please."

"Hello." A young man's voice sounds over the line.

"This is Detective Jolett."

"My name is Gary." He takes a deep breath. "My mother died last night, and my father said you are the detective on the case."

"I am." He makes an audible sound of distress, and then I hear him crying. "I'm sorry for your loss, Gary. I know this can't be easy. I'll answer any questions you have if I have those answers."

"She." He stops. "She told me if she ever died under strange circumstances, I needed to tell the police that it was my father." He pauses, but before I can say anything, he continues with, "Stepfather."

This was the last thing I expected him to say. "When did you have this conversation with your mother?" I ask as I pull my notepad from my pocket and write in it.

"About a year ago. I asked her if he was hurting her, and she said no. She just said I should be aware that he could kill her if something bad happened."

"What did you think when she told you this?"

"I said Dad would never hurt her much less kill her. She told me to remember what she said. After that, we never spoke of it again." He takes a few deep breaths. "My dad said she died in her sleep. She's not old enough to die in her sleep."

Technically, that isn't true. "I'm treating this as a homicide, but as of now, I don't have evidence or reason to suspect anything but accidental death."

"I'm giving you a reason."

I wait a beat before replying, "Do you know if your mother called the police on your father at any point for any reason?" I will be running a criminal history on Mr. Ledmen one way or another, but Gary is helping me connect dots.

"Not that I'm aware of." His voice is calmer now. "I moved out after I graduated high school. I know this sounds crazy. I just somehow think my dad is responsible." He starts crying again, and we end our conversation after I tell him I'll call with any news.

I look at Gabe after disconnecting. "Son says mom warned about dad possibly killing her. I need to see if Mrs. Ledmen was having an affair at the motel or if her husband had someone on the side. It would make a better motive than a fight."

"If it is a homicide, it could have just been the fight."

Gabe and I both know this. We've seen it before. "Why leave the toaster on the floor with water coming out of it?" I don't wait for an answer and continue. "I didn't see the water at first. Mr. Ledmen said he saw the toaster on the floor. None of this adds up, and why would you stick a toaster in the toilet and not start a bath." I pause again and think for a minute. "You force her in the tub, pick up the toaster, drop it in, and it's over. For him to want to electrocute her using the toilet, it means there's underlying hatred of some sort. It doesn't add up."

"What about suicide?"

I'd considered it. "I need to speak to the son again and actually interview him. He'll know more about his mother's more private medical history. Her doctor's name is on her medication and I'll subpoena those records."

"Sounds like you don't need me." The corner of his lips tip.

"Nope, don't need you at all. I have my trusty partner Bell to keep me safe and come up with better suggestions than you. I also need to get home and spend some time with her before she puts in a transfer request."

Gabe stands. "I'll snap her up if she does it. You've been warned."

Chapter Nine

Ick

On day three, I call each person who stayed at the motel that night and speak with them. There was no one in the room on the other side of the Ledmens. I called Sveta and asked if she saw any men hanging out at the room when Mr. Ledmen went to work. Sveta said she never saw anyone. I then examined my photos from the scene along with the recorded interview with Mr. Ledmen. Unfortunately, nothing jumps out and says search here for answers. Bell watches the interview from her blanket but has no advice to offer either.

I jot down questions for Gary, Mrs. Ledmen's son, and call him when I think I have what I need. I can tell he's been crying as soon as he answers.

"I don't have anything new, but I do have

questions that might help me in my investigation if this is a good time."

He sniffs. "I'll tell you anything I can to help."

"Does your father know you're speaking to me?"

"No, and I think I would rather you call him my stepfather." Gary really thinks his stepfather did this.

"I will, Gary. Do you know if your mother spoke to anyone else about her fear of your stepfather?"

"She didn't have friends, really. My stepdad traveled a lot, and she hated being home alone. She was never someone who went for groups. She worked on a few crafts, but that was it. I was glad she was going on this trip."

"Do you know if your stepfather was previously arrested for any type of violence?"

"He got in a bar fight once and was arrested for being drunk and disorderly. My mom was pissed. That was like maybe five years ago. Nothing besides that."

It would show on the criminal history along with anything Gary might not know. My next question was vital, and I was afraid it would close Gary down. "Did your mother suffer from depression?"

Gary didn't hesitate in his answer. "She suffered for years, maybe her entire life. It was more like sadness really. My dad and I hated those times."

He didn't use stepdad and now I know he has feelings for him even if he's worried he killed his mother. You don't instantly stop loving someone.

"Do you know if she ever tried to commit suicide?"

This time he hesitates. "She used pills once. That's the only time I know of. She was hospitalized."

"How long ago was this?"

"Maybe three years but she promised me she would never do it again, and I believed her. She was sad mostly when my dad was away."

"Did your parents argue frequently?"

"Almost never."

"Do you think they had a happy marriage?"

"My mom loved him, and I thought he loved her." Gary's voice muffles slightly, and he's crying again.

"Is there any reason your father would harm your mother? Any reason no matter how small that you can think of?"

"Life insurance. It's all I thought about last night."

"Do you know how much life insurance?"

"I know they had the same policy for years, but a few months ago, my mom had to get a physical for a new policy. She said my dad wanted to be sure she was taken care of if anything happened to him. She wanted a joint policy so he was taken care of too. It was for a million dollars."

Bingo. Motive.

I steered Gary away from the topic of life insurance and hoped it would keep his mind off it after we ended the call. Gary said he would let me know if he thought of anything else, and the interview ended.

"Bell," I say sincerely. "I'm pretty sure we have a homicide." She blinks a few times and closes her eyes. She knows I have paperwork to do, and she's giving me a chance to catch up. She's generous that way.

I need to see if I can get an arrest warrant before Mr. Ledmen leaves town. I run both Mary and her husband's criminal history and while I'm at it, I run their son's. I need a circular look at their family. Mr. Ledmen's one arrest shows and other than Gary having a traffic ticket, he and his mother are clean.

I write my initial report, which includes the interview with Mr. Ledmen. My second report has the autopsy details and the third, my interview with Gary. When I'm done, I call Samantha at the county attorney's office.

"I want to go back in the motel room, and I thought you would like a peek. I may have enough for an arrest warrant. I just don't know how the murder was actually committed and want to run everything past you."

"Do you have a written report?" Nothing happens without paper. No arrest warrants, search warrants, etc.

"In hand and ready for you. I can drop it at your office and drive you to the motel."

"I like your thinking. Give me fifteen

minutes and I'll be ready."

I picked her up exactly fifteen minutes later. Samantha removes her suit jacket before getting in the vehicle. She's in her fifties with graying hair, kept short and styled perfectly. "You still working with psycho dog?" she asks once she's comfortable.

"Bell has her moments, but she is not psycho."

Samantha laughs. "I saw her take down several grown men in training at the park once. She only responds to you when it's time to call her off. She's your dog, and it isn't meant with disrespect, though I am a cat person."

I can see the little old cat lady in her or at least how it will be after she's retired. She'll make a good cat lady. "No offense taken. Bell knows her job." I don't add what a softy Bell really is. If Samantha saw her with Sugarplum, the mop living next to me, she would revise her opinion of Bell to that of a pathetic pile of mush.

We pull up to the motel, and I head inside to grab a key. I called Sveta before picking up Samantha, and she said the room was vacant until she could get the electrical problem fixed. I'd given her a heads-up after talking to the electrician. Once I have the key, we enter the room. It smells clean but more of a disinfectant clean than anything else. The bed is made.

"She was in the bed," I tell Samantha and point my flashlight at the right side of the bed.

"You said she was wet or at least the bedding was."

I stare at the bed. "It was wet, and her clothing was slightly damp too. I got some on the knee of my pants and figured it was urine."

"Your knee?" The look on her face says she doesn't handle gunk well.

"To roll the body, I had to get on the bed, and my knee got wet. I never smelled urine or excrement."

"Is it possible she died in the bathroom and was carried to the bed?"

"It's possible. The bathtub was dry though, and as I tried telling you before, the toilet was the only water source unless he wiped things down after tossing a toaster into the bathtub."

"It could have gone down that way."

"Maybe, but why leave the toaster on the floor with water leaking from it?"

"Homicides never add up. There are always loose ends."

I know that too. The movies have everything adding up perfectly. When homicide happens in real life, detectives look outside the box because a case is never perfect. When it appears that way, something else is usually happening.

"This case has too many loose ends. Nothing adds up."

"Walk me through everything from start to finish," Samantha requests.

For the next hour, we go through the entire case, backtracking through the room when one thing leads to another. We concentrate on suicide first and then switch gears to homicide. It's frustrating because nothing jumps out and says, "Clue!"

At the door, I take a final look at the inside of the room. It holds no more answers.

"What are you thinking?" Samantha asks.

SUZIE IVY

I say nothing as I walk to the side of the bed where Mrs. Ledmen's body was laying. Bending slightly, I pull back the covers and then the mattress pad. The smell of disinfectant hits my nostrils before I make out the darker outline of Mrs. Ledmen's body left by the water or whatever was on the bed.

"They didn't change out the mattress." Everything inside me is fighting not to vomit. "It appears that when someone dies in a motel room and possibly wets the bed, no new mattress is required."

"I'm never sleeping in a hotel again."

My voice is slightly high-pitched. "Maybe hotels are better than motels."

"You know you'll check the mattress before lying down in a bed other than your own."

I shake my head, and we walk outside inhaling the fresh air deeply. "I like your first idea better. I'm never staying in a hotel or motel again."

I don't say a word to Sveta when I return the key. I doubt the health department or any city department has rules about mattresses and dead bodies.

Ick.

Chapter Ten

Paving the Way

On Tuesday, I received an early morning call from Mr. Ledmen. I purposely didn't call him with information or updates. If it were my spouse, I'd be on the phone with the police daily for answers. That's me.

"Detective Jolett, I haven't heard from you," he says with a bit of ire in his voice.

"Hi, Mr. Ledmen. Unfortunately, I have nothing new to report."

He doesn't question me on that. "When will I be able to get my wife's body? I'm having her taken back to Texas."

"I believe the body was released. I'm sorry the mortuary didn't contact you." I wasn't sure if they would call him or not.

"Do you know what killed her?"

"I'm waiting on toxicology. That could take another week." Samantha refused to give me an arrest warrant. I understood her reasoning even if I didn't agree.

"Can I leave town?"

Most people think a police officer or detective can make them stick around. It's more Hollywood crap and not the way it actually is. A judge can make you stay inside city limits; an officer or county attorney cannot.

"You are totally free to leave. I'm sure you want to be with family at this time."

"I want to see my son. He needs me right now."

I was betting the recent conversations between the two of them were not what Mr. Ledmen was hoping for. His son might not have outright accused him of murder, but it would be hard for Gary to hide his anger.

"I should be officially done with my investigation as soon as the toxicology comes back." I also needed Mrs. Ledmen's medical records which I'd subpoenaed. Once I had everything in hand, I would pay another visit to Samantha. The call ended.

Bell came to my side. She senses when I'm stressed or upset. Scratching her head, I run the case past her again. I swear she rolls her eyes when I'm finished. "You have all the answers trapped in that big head of yours, but you never like to share. It's not like I'll steal your glory." She licks my hand and pushes her body against me. I lean over and kiss the top of her head.

Six days later I had the tox report and Mrs. Ledmen's medical records. One report of attempted suicide and prescriptions for anti-depressants and anti-anxiety meds. The toxicology showed alcohol and the prescription drugs I found on the motel dresser.

I call Dr. Thomas.

"This is Detective Jolett. I wanted to talk to you about the toxicology report you sent over."

"Good afternoon, Detective Jolett. I penned your name on my list and planned to call you before heading home today. Do you have any additional information on your case?"

This isn't sounding good, and all I can do is tell him about the son's call. He doesn't sound any happier than I am when he replies.

"Nothing I have will absolutely say Mrs. Ledmen was electrocuted, and her case will be listed as accidental overdose."

"Were there enough drugs in her body to back that theory?"

"Unfortunately, yes. The combination of prescription meds and alcohol are a very possible cause of death. I wish I could help you more."

I couldn't let this go. "Nothing as far as the tissue samples?"

"Nothing out of the ordinary and I spoke with the lab myself."

"I think he killed her." I let that rest for a moment.

Dr. Thomas' voice dropped. "I think he did too."

Today was not turning into the best day. I write up my cause for arrest and decide to tackle Samantha and see if I can get a warrant.

I don't call first, hoping I will catch her in her office. I get lucky. I hand her my file, and she starts looking through it. When she finishes, she glances up. "You know this could be a suicide."

"Then Mr. Ledmen covered it up, and he can explain it once he's in custody."

"Or lawyers up," she says tightly. "I'll get you the arrest warrant, but I want him interviewed before he's in custody. You'll be flying to Texas tomorrow if my secretary can book a flight. Call local law enforcement and let them know you're coming. You won't have your warrant in hand, so they'll make the actual arrest once your home, if the interview goes as planned."

I lean back in my chair, thinking. "He's not going to admit he did it."

She grins. "Of course not, but all I need is a change in his story. Your case is built on circumstantial evidence." She taps my case file against her desk. "His next statements will add to it."

Now it's my turn to grin back. "He'll change his story. I'm sure of it."

An hour later, I'm booked on a flight to

Texas at three the following afternoon. I'll stay in a hotel and interview Mr. Ledmen the day after. Mr. Ledmen lives in the city, and after speaking with a detective in his jurisdiction, the detective sent a police cruiser by to check if anyone was at Mr. Ledmen's house. The detective called me back and assured me he was home.

Chapter Eleven

Full Circle

Bell wasn't traveling with me, so I called Jack, her original trainer. He lived in the city and had watched Bell on another trip I took out of town. I felt comfortable leaving her with Jack, and it also gave the two of us a chance to catch up. We were friends and sometimes I hoped for something more, but it wasn't in the cards. Jack lived four hours away, and he was in charge of the state K9 program for law enforcement. He had no intention of leaving his job and for the first time in a long time, I enjoyed mine and also didn't want to leave.

"Sure. Bell can hang out here for as long as you need. How's she doing?"

"Working homicide doesn't give her enough to do. I feel like she's wasted."

Jack laughs. "I'm sure she's doing fine.

You're too hard on yourself. Dogs are pack animals and just want to be with you."

"She's a very expensive pack animal with very expensive training," I say stubbornly.

"She'll be there when you need her," he says just as stubbornly.

"I'll see you tomorrow at around one. That will give me time to check in for my flight at the airport."

"See you then." I hear the smile in his words. In a different life, Jack would be the perfect man.

I'm asleep by ten. The next few days will be long and traveling never helps. My phone wakes me an hour after I close my eyes.

"Hello." I didn't check the caller ID.

"Dispatch calling. We have a barricade situation with children, and the chief requested you and David 16 on-scene."

My entire body tenses. "What's the location?" She gives me an address, and I recognize it somewhere in the back of my mind.

"Do you have a name on the suspect?"

"Daryl Lewis."

My blood runs cold. I know Daryl, and I also know his ex-wife. She left him after a domestic violence call, I took two years ago. If Melody hadn't left him, I was going to CPS to start the process of removing the two children from their home. Melody surprised me though. She requested a restraining order and wouldn't even allow him to see the kids until he went to therapy. Daryl wasn't happy after going to counseling and not being allowed back into his home. I knew this because we were called out several times. I have no idea how many times he's been arrested for breaking the restraining order.

"How bad is it?" I ask.

"We think he shot his wife. She was able to call 9-1-1, but we haven't heard anything since officers arrived. The suspect came to the door with a gun."

"I'll be there in ten minutes."

Bell whines from the bottom of the bed. Suii helped with the first call I took to this house. If I were lucky, this would go the same way. It was time for Bell to earn her dog chow, and I wasn't feeling good about it. A K9's job is to protect its handler, and they will give their life to do it. I can't go through this again.

Twelve minutes later, with shaking hands and a knot in the pit of my stomach, I arrive on-scene. Police cars surround the house, their strobe lights lighting the entire area. Sergeant Spence approaches me immediately. "Suit up and have Bell on standby. Lewis has his wife and kids at gunpoint. The wife has been shot but from what we know, she's still conscious." He looks to the house before turning back to me. "I've contacted the county for a hostage negotiator, and theirs isn't available. You have your cert, don't you?"

"I do, but I haven't had reason to use it."

"I need you to talk him outside. We need him away from the wife and kids. I have a team on the back door, and they will enter if I give the word. Bell may need to take him down on the porch."

The knot in my stomach turns into a rock. Melody and her kids are in serious danger, and my thoughts are all for Bell. If she attacks Daryl and he lifts his gun, the officers will shoot, and Bell will die.

Sgt. Spence reads the fear in my eyes. "This is her job, Jolett. We need her."

I take a deep breath and nod. I can't do this again, but I have no choice. "Get me a microphone and I'll see if I can talk him out. Where do you want me and Bell?"

"We'll use the microphone from the side car over there." He points to the car at the far right of the fanned-out vehicles. "Let me know when you're ready. I'll alert the guys now," he says next and squeezes my upper arm.

I wanted him to tell the guys not to shoot Bell, but I don't do it. This is Bell's job, and she's trained for this scenario. We'd worked countless hours, and she is more than capable of taking down a man with a gun. My brain flashes to Suii, and I see him making the leap that saved my life. I also see him go down. There was nothing I could do as I watched him take his last breaths. I never even had the chance to tell him thank you.

I open the back hatch of the SUV. "Stay,"

I tell Bell when she tries to jump down. Grabbing her muzzle, I bring my face close to hers and look into her eyes. "I love you, Bell. Stay safe and go home with me tonight, okay?" Her long tongue comes out and slurps the entire length of my face, catching a tear or two on its path. I give her head a squeeze and release her. She knows her job, I tell myself. We can do this.

I grab the duffel bag I need and start gearing up in my SWAT attire. I wasn't officially on the SWAT team but once I acquired Bell, SWAT had me out with them on several suspected explosive calls. She found an inactive pipe bomb for them once, and they think Bell's the bomb. I guess that's SWAT humor.

I don't grab my rifle. I can't fire it while controlling Bell, but I can use my handgun. After suiting up, I clip Bell's leash to her collar and have her jump down. Keeping low, I stay behind the vehicles and approach the one farthest to the right. Leo is behind his car and gives me a thumbs-up. "I'll have your back," he says when I open his door and take a seat behind the wheel. I continue ducking down behind the dashboard and grab his vehicle microphone, clicking the toggle that controls it to loudspeaker. A sharp screech sounds because I didn't turn off my lapel mike.

"Rookie," Leo says from the side of the vehicle. It was a rookie move, and for some reason, it relaxes me.

I smile but keep my attention in front of us while turning my lapel mic off. A low growl comes from Bell, and I tell her no. She knows this is serious, and she doesn't like Leo coming closer. "You're good," I tell him who looks at Bell with surprise. "Move into position." Bell is in the down position on the ground beside me. Leo moves in so he's inside the vee of the door, his feet practically touching Bell. She quickly looks him up and down before turning her eyes back to me. Leo places the barrel of his rifle on the window, pointing at the house.

Bell stays quiet this time. Once Leo is set, I lift the mic again. "This is Detective Laci Jolett. I need to speak with you, Mr. Lewis." I wait ten seconds and try again. "Can you hear me, Mr. Lewis? No one needs to get hurt. I know you love your children. Come onto the porch and talk to me."

Nothing happens for about sixty seconds. Before I lift the microphone again, a chair crashes through the front window. Glass flies and police rifle sights reposition. Bell growls, and I place my hand on her head to steady her. We wait, listening for sounds coming from inside the house. Bell is on high alert, waiting for my command.

"Jolett!" a male voice yells from inside the house.

"I'm here," I call over the loudspeaker. "Come out on the porch and talk with me."

"I'm not coming out to be eaten by your crazy dog."

He must be talking about Suii who took Daryl down during a domestic call more than two years before. "Did you read in the newspaper? My dog was shot and killed." I ask. If he doesn't know about Bell, we might get lucky.

His laughter is downright freaky. "Yeah, I do remember hearing that. Poor doggy. Did you cry?"

The jerk. He's pushing my buttons, and

that is not how I negotiate. "Are your kids okay, Mr. Lewis? I know you don't want to hurt them." When I ran into Melody at the store one day, she told me her ex never hit the kids. She said she finally left him because he beat her up in front of their children. I worried about Melody, but her kids had a better chance of getting out of the house than she did. One thing I do know, Melody loves her kids and will gladly give her life for them. I hope it doesn't come to that.

"You want the kids, come get 'em," Lewis shouts from inside the house.

"That's not how this works, Mr. Lewis. Bring the children onto the porch, and we'll talk."

"Make me."

The passenger door of the patrol car opens, and Sgt. Spence jumps in. "I don't think he likes you. I forgot you had a run-in with him when you had Suii."

"He doesn't care for me. I don't think he knows about Bell, though. If I can hide her at the corner of the house, it's only about ten feet to the porch. If someone can get him to come outside, she can take him down." Yes,

I heard what I was saying. My heart landed somewhere in my stomach region, and I felt sick.

"I'll take over if you want to get into position."

"Be safe, I've got your six," Leo says when I exit the car.

"Don't shoot my nine if at all possible." I gently tug Bell's leash and the two of us run for the side of the house. Denise is stationed on the corner of the garage, and I notice another officer at the back of the side yard. There are no windows on this side of the house, and it's possibly the safest place for a rookie.

She looks at me with nervous eyes, larger than they usually appear. I don't tell her not to shoot Bell because I don't want her hesitating if she needs to take a shot. Leo is well-trained and he's part of the county SWAT team. He'll do his best not to shoot Bell, but he'll do his job first. That job is to keep Melody and the kids safe.

"You okay?" I ask Denise.

Her breath is slightly airy when she speaks. "I'm good."

"Work on your breathing and remember tunnel vision." Tunnel vision is something you learn in the academy, and it's hard for rookies and sometimes even difficult for seasoned officers. When adrenaline pumps through the body, it slows the fine motor skills. Focus becomes a small tunnel. If it's bad, you don't notice what's outside the tunnel, and that will get you killed.

I tap my mic. "In place."

"Mr. Lewis. This is Lou Spence with the police department. We have an ambulance here for your wife and kids. No one wants them hurt. Come out and talk to us."

"My wife isn't leaving here alive. If I go down, she goes down."

I tap my mic, remember it isn't on and make the adjustment. "Focus on the kids," I tell the sergeant.

"Mr. Lewis. I know you don't want to hurt your children. Send them out, and we can talk."

Everything goes quiet, and we wait. If nothing happens, Sgt. Spence will try again in five minutes.

"Movement at the door," sounds in my

earpiece. The door opens, and Mr. Lewis comes out with his arm wrapped around his daughter so she's in front of him. There's no sign of the boy. I remember the little girl though; she's more than two years older now. She's crying and holding on tightly to her father in terror.

"Have her step off the porch, or I can have an unarmed officer come up and get her. Whatever works best for you, Mr. Lewis."

"Stay back." Lewis raises a gun that he was holding at his side. His daughter screams.

I unclip Bell's lead and gently rub her head. I need the girl off the porch for this to work.

"Whatever you want, Mr. Lewis. How can we help?"

"My son stays with me, but you can have the girl." He suddenly pushes his daughter to the ground. She tries to scramble up, but he kicks her. So much for not wanting to hurt his children. The little girl rolls and half falls off the porch. He kicks her again, and she lands on the ground after a three-foot drop.

"Take the lead. Attack," I say into Bell's ear. My heart freezes when Bell silently races for the porch; her muscled body has one goal and that's the gun in Mr. Lewis' hand. His attention isn't on our side of the house. He turns at the last possible moment and sees ninety pounds of killer K9 heading straight for him. His gun comes up, and I know Bell won't survive. She lets out a terrifying growl when she launches herself into the air. Her body slams into his, and her massive teeth grab his wrist. The gun flies. I'm already running, and everyone else has the same thought. I reach the gun first and kick it off the porch while continuing my forward run. One gun means there might be two. Denise is behind me. "Cover the little girl," I yell over Mr. Lewis' screams. Bell has him on his back with her teeth in his upper shoulder close to his throat. Her jaws are now that of a Pitbull when I try to get her off.

"Bell, release," I command. She continues shaking her head, doing as much damage as she can. "Bell, release." I pull her away, and she finally lets go. "Good girl," I praise her.

The other officers take over. The house is cleared, and Mrs. Lewis is taken away in an ambulance. She was found in the back room with her son who had no physical injuries. Mrs. Lewis was shot in the hand and said he shot her when she tried to open their front door and get away. Thankfully, she won't need to worry about her ex-husband for many years once he's prosecuted.

"Good job, Detective Jolett," says Sgt. Spence once things calm down.

I pat Bell's head. "She did a good job and saved those kids."

"Yes, she did, but you let her do it, and I'm proud of you."

I look him in the eyes; police lights still light up the area. "I didn't think I could."

Sgt. Spence smiles. "I knew you would."

Chapter Twelve

Questions and Answers

Our eventful night does not keep me from flying to Texas the following day. The drive seems longer than normal, but I'm tired so it shouldn't be a surprise. I only managed two hours of sleep before Bell insisted I wake up and play with her. Or maybe I needed the added time. I really thought I would lose her the night before, and my heart isn't recovering quickly enough.

I pull into the K9 training center and park. I grab Bell from the back along with her travel kit. She's excited and recognizes her old home even if she wasn't so fond of it back then. Within weeks of picking up Bell, her personality changed. The first time I brought her back here, she wouldn't get out of the car. I promised to return, forced her out, and returned the next day. Our next trip was better because she knew I would return for her.

I look around and don't see Jack on the practice field, so I head to the inside kennels. Jack is cleaning out one of the empty kennels which doesn't surprise me.

"I thought you had rookies for that job," I say by way of greeting.

He looks over and smiles. "Hi, Bell, nice of you to bring your human for a visit." Jack is like Brett and prefers the company of animals to people. I can't help but wonder what he thinks about my company but tamp down the thought before it grows.

I offer a genuine smile. "I need to get on the road so please save your insults for after I'm gone."

Jack turns off the water hose and approaches me. He places his hand down for Bell to sniff first. She licks him and then with the same hand, he shakes mine. I don't say a word about the slime, and it wouldn't matter if I did. What's a little dog slime anyway?

"You'll be caring for a hero," I tell him. "Bell saved two kids and their mom last night so please treat her like royalty. I hate leaving her right now."

Jack is petting Bell again. His head jerks up, and our eyes clash. "Are you okay?"

He understands exactly what Sgt. Spence understood. "I sent her in." I lift my hand to push aside hair that's slid forward on my face and see my hand trembling. Jack notices too.

"You both did your job, and that's what matters." He's always been pragmatic. He steps away, and I go to my knees at Bell's side. "Tell him you get extra cookies before bed."

"I promise," Jack agrees.

I stand and shake his hand again. "Thanks for this. I don't worry when she's with you."

"I've got your K9's back. Stay safe."

The next leg of my trip was a one-hour drive to the airport. I boarded soon after making it through security and was able to study my case file again on the plane and outline my questions for Mr. Ledmen. I was tired and the words blurred, but sleep wouldn't come. I already missed Bell. With a sigh, I go back to my file and continue scribbling notes.

There was a slim window that I might be there for Mr. Ledmen's arrest. I hoped so. There was nothing like the satisfaction of solving a crime and taking a suspect into custody. If it doesn't happen that way, I'll at least live with the knowledge Mr. Ledmen won't be hurting anyone else.

I arrive at the Dallas Fort Worth Airport and take a cab to the hotel booked by the county attorney's office. Once I'm in the room, I eye the bed with disgust. Before I do anything else, I pull back the bedding and check the mattress. No marks to indicate someone died in the bed. It still feels dirty, but there's nothing I can do about it. In one of my evidence collection classes, a trainer told us she sleeps in a sleeping bag when she stays in a hotel room and will not get between the sheets. I understand her thinking now. A sleeping bag sounds wonderful right now. With one last shudder, I click those thoughts off and order room service. After it arrives and I finish my hamburger, I take a shower followed by a final review of my case file. I turn off the light, scramble between sheets that give me the heebie jeebies, and fall into a fitful sleep. Thoughts of body gunk and men with guns hurting Bell fill my dreams.

In the morning, I eat breakfast then call the local police detective I spoke with yesterday and let him know I'm headed in. He put two patrol officers on Mr. Ledmen's house, and he is still home. I need Mr. Ledmen to drive his car to the police station and understand he can leave at any time he wants. If I have no intention of making an arrest, I don't need to read him his Miranda rights. Miranda law changes regularly, but right now, case law says I'm good with this approach.

I give my name to the clerk at the front desk of the police department, and a minute later, Detective Maltos walks out. The detective appears to be in his thirties which is young at most departments. He's about six inches taller than me and wearing slacks and a white dress shirt. His dark hair is cut with military precision, and like so many officers, he gives off the vibe. I follow him to his office, and I share more information about my case.

"This is one for the record books," the detective says after I lay things out for him.

"It is." I'm ready for this case to be over. I want a good night's sleep and with Bell at the foot of the bed. I might even take some time off when this case concludes.

Detective Maltos shows me to the interview room to wait for Mr. Ledmen. Twenty minutes after my arrival, he's shown inside. His eyes flash in my direction, and he doesn't appear happy.

"Hi, Mr. Ledmen," I say and place my hand out. "I've finished the investigation into your wife's death, and I'd like to review my findings with you."

"You came all this way to tell me your findings?" he asks skeptically as his eyes dart around the room. He knows something is off, but I'm ready for this question.

"We're a small department and always have money left in the budget at the end of the year. I insist on giving my cases a personal touch." I lay it on thick and keep talking so he doesn't have a chance to think

SUZIE IVY

about what I'm saying. "Did your son tell you I spoke with him a few days ago?"

His eyes meet mine, his expression guarded. "He said you called."

"I did. I wanted to know a few things about your wife from his point of view. It was enlightening. Why don't we have a seat, and we'll go over what I have."

"You don't need me, so I'll wait in my office," Detective Maltos says.

I open my file as soon as the door closes and pull out a picture of Mrs. Ledmen's right hand with the burns. While Mr. Ledmen's brain scrambles to figure out what's going on, I want to hear his first response. I push the picture in front of him. "Can you explain this burn on the back of your wife's hand?"

He looks at the picture and picks it up. His hand starts shaking. "She burned it on the hot plate," he finally says.

Original.

"What about this one?" I place the picture of her foot in front of him.

He tears his eyes away from the picture before responding. "She bought a new pair of sandals, and the strap rubbed her foot.

She insisted on wearing them even with the cold weather. They caused a rug burn on her foot, and she still wore them until her foot looked like it was becoming infected."

The lies roll so easily off his tongue. He's had time to plan. "Was the burn on her hand treated by a doctor?" I ask quickly.

He shakes his head. "No, but we went to the pharmacy in town for burn medication."

Our local pharmacy has video, and they might still have recordings of the days prior to Mrs. Ledmen's death. "Did you find medication that helped?"

"We weren't sure what to use so we spoke to the pharmacist. He was an older man with a bald head."

The description, as vague as it is, describes our pharmacist Miles Atkinson. I need to call him.

"What is this about?" Mr. Ledmen asks with a flash of irritation.

I can't give away my new thoughts, so I give him what I planned before I arrived. "The toaster had water in it, and I suspect your wife might have tried to kill herself."

He lets out a long breath. "I was worried about that too," he says. I also notice a loosening of his shoulders. He's relieved I'm going down this path.

"Did you suspect suicide when you found her on the floor?"

"Absolutely not. I thought she passed out like she has many times before. After I found her dead, I used the bathroom. That's when I noticed the toaster. I almost picked it up, but I didn't notice the water. She promised our son she would never try to kill herself again. I hoped she would keep that promise."

I desperately wanted to talk to the pharmacist. "I'm sorry, Mr. Ledmen, but I need to use the ladies' room. Could you excuse me? It will only be a few minutes if someone is around to show me where it is." I've used this excuse a thousand times when I need to leave a suspect in the interview room and check out a story.

Detective Maltos waits outside the room. He's been monitoring the interview. "Do you think he's telling the truth?"

"I don't know. He seems to have all his answers ready. It didn't feel this way when I interviewed him directly after his wife's death. I need to call our pharmacy and see if I can talk to the person who helped him find the burn cream."

I had the phone number in my cell and called from Detective Maltos' office. "Hi," I say to the woman who answers. This is Detective Jolett. Is Miles Atkinson available for a quick question. It's urgent."

"Hold please." I hope she understands the word urgent.

A minute later, Miles picks up the phone. "This is Miles Atkinson, how may I help you, Detective Jolett?"

"Thank you, Mike. I have a question. By any chance, do you remember a husband and wife in their forties coming into the pharmacy about a week ago?"

Before I continue, he replies, "A lot of couples in their forties come into the pharmacy."

"This couple was looking for burn cream for the wife's hand."

"Oh, I remember that. They were staying at the motel and a hot plate fell off the counter and hit the back of her hand."

My case is unraveling quickly. "Do you

remember seeing the actual burn?"

"It was nasty, and I suggested they seek medical attention, but they refused."

"Did you think anything was strange about the encounter?"

"Not at all. I was impressed the woman wasn't screaming in pain, but they were both pleasant."

"Thank you for your time." I hung up, bringing my eyes to Detective Maltos. "Remember that case that would be one for the record books?" I don't wait for his reply. "It just fell to pieces."

Chapter Thirteen

Putting Everything Together

I took my beating once I returned to my department. At least Detective Maltos was generous in his lack of teasing, and for that I was thankful.

Lou Macky entered my office an hour after I came to work. He was carrying two large coffees. "I figured you needed this," he said with a grin.

"Get it over with, please. My day is not going well."

"Death by toaster. Only you could mess up a case that bad."

"Har, har."

"No, seriously. The toaster wasn't talking, and somehow you managed a full confession."

I pick up a piece of paper, crumple it, and

throw it at him. "Kill," I told Bell and point at Lou.

She doesn't budge, and Lou laughs all the way out of my office. I go back to my paperwork until my phone rings.

"I have Gary Ledmen on the phone for you. He says it's concerning his mother's case."

"Thank you, please put him through."

"Hello, this is Gary Ledmen."

"Hi, Gary, how may I help you?"

"You don't think my father killed my mother, do you?"

"I'm sorry, Gary, but I don't have evidence that a crime was committed."

"He killed her. I know he did it. He wanted the money, and he already has a new girlfriend."

This gives me pause. "If you have additional information, at any time, I will re-open the case and review it. Anything," I say softly.

"He's going to get away with killing my mother."

"If I had proof, I would charge him with murder, but I have no proof."

"He did it." I hear the soft click of the receiver when he hangs up.

I thought my day couldn't get worse. An hour before I was ready to go home, Stanley Conners enters my office. I really want to give Bell a treat after she lifts her head, bares her teeth, and growls at him. I snap my fingers, and she meanders to my side while keeping her eyes on Stanley.

"How may I help you, Officer Conners?"

"I heard how you screwed up your murder case."

I silently count to ten. "Enlighten me. How did I screw up my murder case?"

This catches him off guard. "I've heard the rumors."

I relax. He's here fishing, and I'll be darned if I take his bait. "The case is concluded and public record if you'd like to review my procedures. Write up your findings and turn them in to Sergeant Spence. I'm sure he'll give you kudos for solving it your way."

"I'll share my findings with my father too," he tosses out, still on the hunt.

"You do that. I'm sure it will give him

something to do outside his city council seat. If he can do better, you might suggest he go to the police academy. We need good officers who move up the chain of command without daddy paving the way." Stanley's face goes red so I keep flapping my lips, unable to help myself. "Just let him know his city council job pays more, and he might want to raise our pay before switching careers." Stanley is an obnoxious bully, and Bell gives another low growl. "Bell is hungry, and she's looking at you like a piece of steak. You need to leave my office. I'll inform records to pull a copy of the case for you. Please review it on your own time so the department isn't paying for you to check my work."

Stanley decides he has someplace else he needs to be.

∞∞∞∞

The following week, Bell and I take time off. The weather is decent, and we're able to take a long hike through our favorite area. It's my chance to review the case with her and share my thoughts.

"Mr. Ledmen killed his wife, Bell. I don't know how he did it, and there's nothing I can do. I reviewed every detail a hundred times. One of the pictures had a tube of burn cream in it." We keep walking, and Bell stays silent, except for her panting from the long hike which blends with the sounds of nature. "The life insurance policy is the key. I sent them a copy of the report, and he's getting the money. He's completely out of our jurisdiction now and most likely I'll never see him again. It's just not right, and the feeling that I missed something won't go away."

Bell notices something ahead and pulls at the lead. I unsnap it and let her run. She wasn't helping me with the Ledmen case anyway.

I hear Gary's voice in my head when I try to sleep. He's convinced his stepdad committed murder, and so am I. The only thing I can do is check in on Mr. Ledmen from time to time. Maybe if he did it once, he'll do it again. I already feel sorry for that poor woman.

Bell comes galloping back with a stick in her jaws. I toss it for her, and she takes off.

A short while later, we find a spot to eat our lunch. I brought a few treats for Bell. She munches them down and gives me her sad face when I show her my empty hand.

"Be careful or you'll grow fat and lazy," I tell her.

She gives a short whine then crawls toward me and licks my hand.

It's detective work; we don't always get our man, but if we have a K9, slobber is a close runner-up.

∞∞∞

The Next installment in the **Forever Series**, The Forever Friend, available NOW!

A note from Suzie,

I wrote the first half of The Forever Partner six years ago. The file name on my computer was DBT, Death by Toaster and it was the account of an actual case that took place about midway through my detective career. As I reread the story, I knew Laci Jolett could handle this case.

Thank you for purchasing and The Forever Partner. Writing is the lonely part of the book process, but publishing takes many people. Thank you, Kim and Laura for your insightful editing, you rock.

My goal in the Laci Jolett books is to give detective realism and what it takes in today's world to solve cases. You don't always get your man or woman. Cases are complex and they never abide by Hollywood rules. The good guys don't always win and the bad guys don't always lose. Such is life. I promise, Laci and Bell do solve crimes and they're ready to go in The Forever Friend and I've included the first chapter below.

Now to Bell. Like Suii, she's a real hero. The K9 I worked with was a black lab just like Bell and I've given her the same traits. She was the greatest police dog ever and it's wonderful to give you a peek inside her career. I have the funniest story about Bell that happened late one night and hope I can include it in the next book.

My, gulp, 50 books are my bread and butter. My other novels consist of paranormal and contemporary romance with bad words and steamy scenes, and great stories. The exception to this rule is my latest Genetically Modified Series which is quite tame on the steam side with bad words missing too. The books are based on the life of Marinah, an incredible young woman who died of an accidental drug overdose at age nineteen. Her mother is one of my readers and friends. I gave Marinah a life in these books. They take place after her family dies as she lives on in a post-apocalyptic world where hellhounds decimate earth. I promise they're worth reading!

Shadow by Holly S Roberts (Book 1)

Visit http://wickedstorytelling.com for a list of all my work

Visit http://suzieivy.com for my mysteries

Thank you so much for reading The Forever Partner!

Suzie

The Forever Friend
Chapter One

The cold nose, low whine, and warm dog breath in my face let me know something was wrong. Bell had a dog door leading out to my small back patio area and it remained open in the summer. It was the middle of our warm season and there was no reason Bell should be waking me at—I peer over to the clock—three a.m. My eyelids slowly peeled partially open as I tried to make sense of Bell's early morning needs.

As soon as she was sure I was awake, she gave a quick high-pitched yap and headed to the bedroom door. Once there, she turned and waited on me.

Bell's behavior was strange. She was highly trained for protection and sniffing out explosives. An odd combination to partner with a homicide detective but it worked for us. I knew if something worried Bell, it needed to worry me. Due to a murder trial at the courthouse, I was mentally tired. Too many hours tied to the courtroom defense chair for the past two weeks.

Most people don't understand the psychological toll a murder trial takes on a detective. From trying to understand the imperial workings of the justice system to passing notes like a grade-schooler trying not to get caught; it's a lesson in perseverance.

The case was one of my first murder arrests as a homicide detective. Last night, I received news from the county attorney's office that the jury was back and the verdict would be read at ten a.m. this morning.

I planned to sleep until eight.

My legs slid to the side of the bed and my feet hit the floor while my vision decided clear was an option.

"Woof." Her 80-pound body of muscle did the dance of impatience.

"I hear you, Bell. I'm trying to wake up," I said while grabbing my shorts from the top of the dresser and slipping them on. My flip-flops were next and I walked from the room with Bell a few feet ahead of me. She went straight for the front door which I didn't expect.

Her hackles weren't raised, and I was unsure what was happening on the other side of the door. She gave me another high-pitched whine when I headed back to my bedroom and grabbed my gun, forcing the holster's belt clip over the waist of my shorts. It was not ideal because the weight of the gun pulled down without a proper belt to secure it, but as an officer, I needed my gun to feel safe with an unknown on the other side of the door. I slipped my cell into my back pocket for added safety.

Once I was armed and ready for what Bell thought needed my attention, I opened the door a few inches. Bell's heavy body hit the wood and forced it from my hand and she charged out. I was too surprised to yell.

Yes, I should have put her leash on, but this was not normal Bell behavior. I watched her run straight for my neighbor's door, and that was when I heard the slight whine and scratching coming from inside Ed's condo.
It was Sugarplum, Ed's mop he called a dog and something was seriously wrong. Leaving Bell at the neighbor's door, I rushed back into my condo and grabbed Ed's spare key off the hook just inside my front door.

My fingers shook as I opened Ed's door and

entered. Bell and Sugarplum did their thing —licking and sniffing.

"Ed," I said loudly. "It's Laci and Bell."

He didn't answer so I headed to the hallway and repeated myself.

Still no reply.

Ed's condo was laid out like mine only mirrored so the master bedroom door was on my right and not my left. I found Ed halfway between the door and his bed, collapsed on the floor. I was dialing 9-1-1 as I checked for a pulse.

Nothing.

"This is Detective Jolett. My neighbor is unresponsive, and I need an ambulance here stat." I read my address aloud though they had it on file and the ambulance crew knew where I lived. "I'm hanging up to begin CPR."

Ed and I hadn't always had the best relationship, and that was on me. I was mean and cranky when I first moved in, and I had no idea I was a dog lover. Maybe dog lover was a little strong. I loved two dogs—Suii, the K9 who gave her life for mine and Bell, my current K9 partner. Ed's little craptsu, Sugar-plum, and I had an agreement. I tolerated her, and she pooped on my lawn with my blessing. Like may be the strongest word I could use with her.

Ed's complexion was death-white. I began chest compressions and prayed the ambulance arrived quickly. His body was warm, and I knew the nighttime dog patrol did its job by alerting me so quickly. I was not in the least surprised Sugarplum notified Bell. I would be surprised if she hadn't. I'd learned dogs had a sixth sense that we didn't quite understand. Bell proved it daily. She was always in tune with my moods and reacted accordingly. On mentally gloomy days, Bell pinned herself to my side and never made a fuss. When I was jumpy or impatient with a case, she threw fits until I took her to the park. During our walks, I could clear my thoughts and unravel or resolve a few of the problems I carried.

Bell understood me like no one else.

After I realized how much Bell responded to my moods, I told Ed. It was difficult for me to put it into words but Ed understood. He told me stories about Sugarplum and several of his previous dogs who did exactly as Bell. I no longer felt stupid for thinking Bell read my mind. I didn't advertise the knowledge and I also didn't discount it.

I finally heard the ambulance in the distance, and I still couldn't find a pulse between the chest compressions I performed. Bell growled when the first EMT charged in the door.

"Bell, down," I told her, and she immediately went to her haunches. "She's good and you can come in," I said hastily. "I'll put her and the little dog in my condo as soon as you take over."

The entire team moved in, eyeing Bell carefully. They'd been around her and they knew she would protect me. They kept a respectful distance and went to work. Paper sleeves, plastic stoppers, and medical jargon was thrown out as they began CPR using better equipment than my hands. I swiped Sugarplum under the belly and lifted her to my side, moving us out of their way. Sugarplum kept her eyes on Ed, and I gave her a little squeeze. I wanted to reassure her, but I knew this wasn't good.

"Come on, Bell. Let's get Sugarplum next door." I left the condo with Bell one step behind.

Ed had a daughter in California. After they took him to the hospital, I'd find her information inside Ed's place.

I looked around my condo and placed Sugarplum on the kitchen floor by Bell's water bowl. Her head hit the top. Chances were good she could jump her front legs up and get to the water if the bowl was filled. One long drink from Bell and Sugarplum wouldn't be able to reach. I grabbed a small bowl out of the cabinet and filled it with water, then placed it next to Bell's.

Sugarplum took a few laps with her tongue, then turned and looked up at me with super sad puppy eyes. I thought she was around six, but her fuzzy white hair and the obnoxious pink bow on her head made me think she was a puppy. Her intelligence was totally on the puppy scale, and she had no manners at all. Of course, her owner was the bigger problem, but he loved her and the two of them were a team.

Part of having Bell assigned to me was that I have no other dog in my house. It had been burned into my brain that she must be the only dog I own. I had no idea why and never asked. I had no intention of having the one dog I currently own. I looked down while Sugarplum's little tail swished back and forth, and she blinked at me in sorrow.

I checked the clock. It was too early to call Jack, the K9 trainer I questioned about all things dog. He was the reason Bell came into my life. After Suii's death, I swore off police dogs. Jack had other ideas and knew Bell and I would be forever partners.

"Woof."

I watched Bell as she looked down on Sugarplum. With a sigh, I picked up the rat again and headed out the front door to see how things were going with Ed. They rolled him past us while still administering CPR.

Roger, one of the EMTs, in his mid-thirties and a nice guy, stopped and asked, "Do you have family information for us?"

"I'll find it after you're clear and I'll bring it to the hospital."

"They're taking him to Mountain General."

The ambulance and EMTs arrived as one and drove off the same way. Now I was alone with a small white rat, Bell, and a sullen quiet. "Good dogs," I told them both softly. I walked into Ed's condo and found his wallet next to his keys on a small table by his front door.

IN AN EMERGENCY CONTACT:

The card was directly behind his license and showed his daughter's name and phone number. I put Sugarplum on the floor and dialed, hoping she answered. Unfortunately, she didn't, and I was forced to leave the bad news in a message. I left my contact information and the name of the hospital. Looking down at poor Sugarplum, I let Ed's daughter know I was taking care of his dog and disconnected. It was a little after four and still too early to call Jack. I gathered food supplies for Sugarplum, picked her back up, and returned to my condo.

Bell nudged my arm when I didn't immediately place Sugarplum down so I lowered her. Bell licked her face, and Sugarplum danced slightly at the attention. The two of them got along, but they'd never been in a confined space together. The repeated kissing helped relieve that worry. It wasn't that Bell would hurt her physically, but if she didn't want the scrappy dog around, she would have no problem growling and making her back off.

Sugarplum decided to check out the house with Bell walking along behind her during the tour. I needed coffee and started a pot. I was fully aware I wouldn't be going back to bed. I pulled dishes from the dishwasher and started putting them away while the coffee dripped and the aroma filled the kitchen. When I turned at the sound of Bell's nails on the kitchen tile, her ears were back and she didn't look happy.

On the other hand, Sugarplum, trailing behind Bell with a tail going ninety miles an hour, was looking quite pleased. I didn't need to be much of a dog person to know what that meant. Bell had no trouble leading me to the nice brown pile left from Sugarplum's tour of my bedroom. I didn't see any wet spots which was the only good thing about the unfortunate situation.

I turned at the sound of Bell's yap. "Oh, don't worry. I know from the size that you hold no responsibility." Bell yapped again, wagged her tail in happiness that she was not being blamed, and went in search of her new friend. I grabbed tissue and disposed of Sugarplum's bad behavior.

Amazon: The Forever Friend

About The Author

Suzie Ivy

 Suzie lives high in the Arizona Mountains with her husband and two spoiled dogs. She's a USA TODAY Bestselling Author of more than fifty books writing under three names. She loves reading, gardening and martial arts and she'll never be too old to go after her dreams.